Lincoln Public Library

December 1976

XALA

also by Sembène Ousmane

GOD'S BITS OF WOOD (LES BOUTS DE BOIS DE DIEU)
LE DOCKER NOIR
LE MANDAT
L'HARMATTAN
O PAYS, MON BEAU PEUPLE
VOLTAÏQUE

XALA

Sembène Ousmane

translated by Clive Wake

LAWRENCE HILL&CO.

Library of Congress Cataloging in Publication Data
Ousmane, Sembène
Xala.
I. Title.
PZ3.09445Xa13   [PQ3989.08]   843   75-41811
ISBN 0-88208-067-9

December 1976

© Editions Présence Africaine, 1974
© in English translation, Heinemann Educational Books
Illustrations taken from Sembène Ousmane's film XALA

First US edition, October, 1976
Lawrence Hill & Company, Publishers, Inc.
24 Burr Farms Road
Westport, Connecticut 06880

Library of Congress Catalog Card Number: 75-41811
ISBN: 0-88208-067-9

Manufactured in the United States of America

1   2   3   4   5   6   7   8   9   10

XALA

The 'businessmen' had met to mark the day with a celebration worthy of the event. Never before in the history of Senegal had the Chamber of Commerce and Industry been headed by an African. For the first time a Senegalese occupied the President's seat. It was their victory. For ten long years these enterprising men had struggled to capture this last bastion of the colonial era from their adversaries.

They had come together from different sectors of the business community to form the 'Businessmen's Group' in order to combat the invasion of foreign interests. It was their ambition to gain control of their country's economy. Their anxiety to constitute a social clan of their own had increased their combativity, tingeing it with xeno-phobia. Over the years they had managed – with some help from the politicians – to obtain a foothold in the wholesale trade, and to a lesser extent in the import and export field. They had become more am-bitious and had tried to acquire a stake in the administration of the banks. In their public statements they had specified those branches of the economy which they felt were theirs by right: the wholesale trade, public works contracts, the pharmacies, the private clinics, the bakeries, the manufacturing industry, the bookshops and cinemas; but their exclusion from the banks had first stimulated then sharpened a nationalist feeling from which expectations of improved social status were not entirely absent.

The appointment of one of their number as President of the Chamber of Commerce and Industry gave them renewed hope. For the men gathered together on this auspicious day, the road was now open that led to certain wealth. It meant access to the heart of the country's economy, a foothold in the world of high finance and, of course, the right to walk with head held high. Yesterday's dreams were beginning to come true. The full significance of what was happening today would be felt in the days to come. Its importance fully justified this celebration.

The Group's President paused in his speech. His eyes shone with satisfaction as they came to rest on each member of his audience in turn: ten or so expensively dressed men. The cut of their made-to-measure suits and their immaculate shirts were ample evidence of their success.

Smiling and relaxed, the President resumed his speech: 'Friends, this is a great occasion. Since the beginning of the foreign occupation no African has ever been President of the Chamber' (Perhaps because of their megalomania, they always referred to the 'Chamber of Commerce and Industry' as 'the Chamber'.) 'In appointing me to this post of great responsibility our government has acted with courage and shown its determination to achieve economic independence in these difficult times. This is indeed an historic occasion. We owe a debt of gratitude to our government and to the man at its head.'

They broke into applause, congratulating themselves on their victory. Calm returned amid coughing and scraping of chairs.

'We are the leading businessmen in the country, so we have a great responsibility. A very great responsibility indeed. We must show that we can measure up to the confidence the government has placed in us. But it is time now to bring this memorable day to a close by reminding you that we are invited to the wedding of our colleague El Hadji Abdou Kader Beye. Although we are anxious to belong to the modern world we haven't abandoned our African customs. I call upon El Hadji to speak.'

El Hadji Abdou Kader Beye, who was seated on the President's right, rose to his feet. His close-cropped hair was streaked with white but he carried his fifty odd years well.

'Friends, at this precise moment (looking at his gold wrist-watch) the marriage has been sealed at the mosque. I am therefore married.'

'Re-re-married. How many times does that make it?' flung out Laye, the Group's humorist, sarcastically.

'I was coming to that, Laye. I have now married my third wife, so I'm a "captain" as we African's say. Mr President, will you all do me the honour of being my guests?'

2

'A fitting way to end the day. Gentlemen, the women are waiting for us. Shall we go?'

The meeting was over.

Outside a line of expensive cars was waiting for them. El Hadji Abdou Kader Beye drew the President to one side: 'Take the head of the convoy. I must go and collect my other two wives.'

'All right.'

'I won't be long,' said El Hadji, climbing into his black Mercedes.

Modu his chauffeur drove off.

El Hadji Abdou Kader Beye had once been a primary-school teacher, but he had been dismissed from the service because of his involvement in trade-union activity during the colonial period. After his dismissal he had acquired business experience in the grocery trade and had then set himself up as a middleman in property transactions. He had made an increasing number of friends among the Lebanese and Syrian businessmen, one of whom became his associate. For nearly a year they had held a monopoly in the sale of rice, a staple commodity. This period of success had placed him way ahead in the ever-growing field of small middlemen.

Then came Independence. By now he had capital and connections, so he was able to set up on his own. He turned his attention to the south, especially the Congo, concentrating on the importation of dried fish. It was a gold mine, until a competitor with better ships and more solid business connections forced him out. He turned his energies towards Europe, with shell-fish. Lack of funds and inadequate financial backing obliged him to abandon this scheme. However, because he was well-known and had a certain standing in the business community, overseas investors paid him to act as a front. He was also on the boards of two or three local companies. He played his various roles well but, although the law was fooled, everyone knew what was really happening.

He was a good, albeit a non-practising Muslim, so on the strength of his growing affluence he took his first wife on the pilgrimage to Mecca. Hence his title of 'El Hadji', and 'Adja' for his wife. He had six children by this wife, the eldest of whom, Rama, was a student at the university.

El Hadji Abdou Kader Beye was what one might call a synthesis of

3

two cultures: business had drawn him into the European middle class after a feudal African education. Like his peers, he made skilful use of his dual background, for their fusion was not complete.

His second wife, Oumi N'Doye, had given him five children. So, to date El Hadji had two wives and a string of progeny. Eleven in all. Each of his families had its own villa. Being a practical African, he had provided a mini-bus for their domestic use and to take the children to their various schools in town.

This third marriage raised him to the rank of the traditional notability; it represented a kind of promotion.

* * *

The reception for this third marriage was being held at the home of the young girl's parents. In this, ancient custom was being more than just respected, it was being revived. The house had been invaded since early morning. Male and female griots welcomed the guests – family, friends, acquaintances – who proceeded to gorge themselves with food and drink. Those among them who claimed royal or noble ancestry spent freely, rivalling one another in generosity, and made great display of their clothes and – among the women – of their head-dresses and jewelry. Boubous spangled with silver and gold thread, gold and silver pendants and bracelets glittered in the sunlight. The wide necklines of the women revealed the shimmering, velvety aubergine of their shoulders. The laughter, the clapping of hands, the soft, melodious accents of the women and the thick tones of the men created an atmosphere of noisy well-being, like the gentle roar from inside a sea-shell.

In the middle of the main room of the house the husband's gifts were displayed in sets of a dozen each on a trestle-table: lady's underwear, toiletries, shoes in various fashions and colours, wigs from blonde to jet black, fine handkerchiefs and scented soaps. The centre-piece was a red casket inside which lay the keys of a car.

The guests clustered round the table, admiring and commenting on these proofs of love. A young woman wearing a heavy gold bracelet turned to her neighbour and remarked: 'As well as the car, El Hadji has promised her 2,500 gallons of five-star petrol.'

'There are strings attached, my dear,' retorted the neighbour, lifting

4

the wide sleeve of her embroidered silk boubou with a gesture of her hand.

'Strings or not, I'd marry El Hadji even if he had the skin of a crocodile.'

'Ah! but you're no longer a virgin, my dear!'

'You think so?'

'What about your children?'

'And what about the Virgin Mary?'

'Don't blaspheme!' the woman objected sulkily, waving a finger in the other's face. For a moment they glared at each other in silent confrontation.

'I was only joking,' said the first woman, in reluctant conciliation.

'I should hope so,' replied the other, who was a Catholic. She smiled in triumph. Then she spoke, gesturing towards the gifts. 'Personally I'd hate to be one of El Hadji's wives.'

'You can make good soup in an old pot,' murmured the other. She ran her fingers over a skirt to see if it was made of silk or terylene.

'Not with new sweet-potatoes,' replied the second.

They shook with laughter and moved off towards another group of women.

Yay Bineta, the 'mistress of ceremonies', otherwise known as the Badyen (the bride's aunt and her father's sister) was keeping a wary eye on things. A dumpy woman with a large behind, a flabby black face and spiteful eyes, she made sure the guests kept their places according to their rank in this welter of individuals. It was she who had given 'her' daughter in marriage for according to traditional law the brother's child is also his sister's daughter.

Some months previously when they had met at a family gathering, the girl's mother had unburdened herself to her sister-in-law (the Badyen is equal in status to the husband). She had told the Badyen quite frankly of her fears. Her daughter had twice failed her elementary certificate; she was now nineteen years old and her parents could not afford to go on paying for her schooling.

'If she cannot find a job,' said the mother, 'it's Yalla's will. (But deep down she thought her daughter had enough education to be a secretary.) She will have to get married. We must find her a husband. She is at the right age. There have never been any unmarried mothers in our family, although these days it is no exaggeration to say that to be an unmarried mother is the height of fashion.'

Old Babacar, the head of the family who had retired from work, agreed with his wife's arguments for he was finding it impossible to keep his large brood of seven children on his tiny quarterly pension.

'Do you have anyone in mind?' Yay Bineta had asked, fixing her narrow, bean-like eyes on her brother.

Old Babacar lowered his eyes with that feigned modesty of men of religion. Nothing had been. . . His wife's authority was limitless. Friends of his own age-group all said that it was Babacar's wife who wore the trousers in the home. The fact too that he had never taken a second wife made him particularly vulnerable to male criticism.

'Yalla is my witness, if N'Gone our daughter had a husband I'd be very happy. But it is all a question of chance, and only Yalla provides that,' he said, speaking with circumspection.

'Yalla! Yalla! You must plough your own field!' retorted his wife angrily as she turned to face Yay Bineta (and in so doing effectively silenced her husband). 'I won't try and hide what kind of young men she goes about with. Until today's sun not a single well-bred, serious, worthwhile man has been to this house. The only ones that come are the sort who don't have a pocket handkerchief and wear clothes only fit for a scarecrow. N'Gone spends all her time going out with them to the cinema and dances. None of them has a job. They're just a lot of loafers. I dread the month when she won't be washing her linen at nights'*.

'I understand,' said Yay Bineta. 'There is a queue of girls waiting for husbands that stretches from here to Bamako. And it is said that the lame ones are in the front.'

Her irony made Babacar laugh, but his laughter stung Mam Fatou, his wife.

'This is women's business,' she said harshly to her husband. Anger began to show at the end of her chin and gathered in her eyes.

Old Babacar meekly withdrew, full of apologies, saying it was time to go and pray. When they were alone Mam Fatou begged the Badyen:

'Yay Bineta, N'Gone is your daughter. You know so many people

* The menstrual period; the linen is never dried in the daytime so as to keep it out of sight of the men.

6

in N'Dakaru. People who could help us. Look how we live, like animals in a yard. And if N'Gone or her younger sister brings us bastard children, what will become of us? The way things are these days chance has to be helped along a little.'

Weeks, then months passed. One morning Yay Bineta dressed N'Gone in her best clothes and they went to El Hadji Abdou Kader Beye's shop, where he also had his office. Yay Bineta and El Hadji had known each other a long time. Yay Bineta immediately set to work to explore the lie of the land.

'El Hadji, this is my daughter N'Gone. Take a good look at her. Could she not be a kind of measure? A measure of length or a measure of capacity?'

'She is gentle. A drop of dew. She is ephemeral too. A pleasant harbour for the eyes,' replied El Hadji, who had been accustomed to using this kind of language since attaining manhood.

'You say "for the eyes". You speak in the plural. I am talking in the singular. One owner only.'

'One-eyed then!' the man laughed, relaxed.

'You don't tell a person with one eye to close it.'

'No more than you need to show the hand how to find the mouth.'

'You have to prepare something for the hand to take to the mouth.'

This was a game in which Yay Bineta was well versed. She did battle with the man in the ancient, allegorical language preserved by custom. N'Gone, the child of national flags and hymns, understood nothing of what they were saying. The contest was interrupted by the ringing of the phone. The Badyen pretended she was looking for a job for her daughter. The man promised to see what he could do. Careful of his reputation for generosity he gave them a thousand francs to pay for a taxi home.

Other visits followed. Conversations that were all the same, with nothing special about them. The Badyen would bait the man: 'You're afraid of women! Your wives make the decisions, wear the trousers in your house, don't they? Why don't you come and see us? Hey? Why don't you?' El Hadji Abdou Kader Beye was wounded in his pride. His honour as an African in the old tradition was being called in question. He was at last stung into taking up the challenge. 'No woman is going to tell me what to do,' he said to himself. And so, to prove that he was master in his own house, he accompanied them to the home of the girl's parents.

And then what happened? N'Gone began to visit him by herself, especially in the afternoon. She said she had come to see if El Hadji had found her a job, an excuse thought up by the Badyen. The man slowly succumbed. A change in his feelings began to take place. He became used to her. He felt a growing desire for her. As her visits continued and settled into regularity, El Hadji took her out to tea shops, occasionally to a restaurant. Once or twice they attended 'businessmen's' cocktail parties.

He had to admit it, N'Gone had the savour of fresh fruit, which was something his wives had long since lost. He was drawn by her firm, supple body, her fresh breath. With his two wives on the one hand and the daily demands of his business life, N'Gone seemed to him like a restful oasis in the middle of the desert. She was good for his pride too – he was attractive to a young woman!

Yay Bineta, the Badyen, kept discreetly out of sight, all the better to direct events. El Hadji Abdou Kader Beye was received in princely style at the girl's home. The food was exquisite and the scent of incense filled N'Gone's small wooden room. Nothing was omitted in the careful process of conditioning the man. The Badyen spun her web as painstakingly as a spider. All the neighbours knew – chiefly from gossip round the public tap – that El Hadji Abdou Kader Beye was courting N'Gone with the most honourable intentions. Skilfully the Badyen got rid of the young men in her daughter's circle. Then the engagement was officially announced.

The fruit was ripe. The Badyen was going to pluck it.

On the day in question El Hadji was to take N'Gone with him to an important reception. The day before he had fitted her out from head to foot in new clothes. Her father, her mother and the Badyen greeted him when he arrived. While they waited for N'Gone to get ready Yay Bineta opened the discussion:

'El Hadji Abdou Kader Beye, you have been to Mecca, the home of the prophet Mohammed – peace be on him and on the whole world. You are a respectable man and we all know your honourable intentions towards N'Gone. We can tell you with certainty that our daughter sees only with your eyes, hears only with your ears. But you know how young she is. The neighbours are gossiping. We are not rich in money, that we cannot deny; but we are decent people, rich in our pride. No one in our family has ever acted dishonourably. We want you to know today that it depends on you alone for N'Gone to be yours for the rest of her life.'

El Hadji was trapped. The thought of marriage had until now never crossed his mind. He had been caught off his guard by the Badyen and could only splutter a reply in the vaguest terms. He must talk to his wives. Yay Bineta realized she had the upper hand. She goaded him. Was he not a Muslim? The son of a Muslim? Why did he try to evade Yalla's obvious wishes? Was he a whiteman that he must consult his wives? Had the country lost its men of yesterday? Those brave men whose blood flowed in his veins?

As always in this kind of exchange, the less aggressive of the two contestants eventually gave in. El Hadji Abdou Kader Beye surrendered out of weakness. There was no way he could use the law of the Koran for his own justification. As for his wives, why should he explain himself to them? All he had to do was tell them.

In the weeks that followed, Yay Bineta speeded up the preparations. Mam Fatou, the girl's mother, seeing the way things were going and the urgency that seemed to possess the Badyen, had certain misgivings. She was deeply opposed to polygamy and wanted El Hadji to repudiate his two wives.

The Badyen was angry with her sister-in-law for her attitude. 'Mam Fatou, get this clear,' she told her, 'El Hadji is a polygamist, but each of his wives has her own house in the best part of town. Each of these houses is worth fifty or sixty times this hovel. And he is such a good match from your point of view! N'Gone's future and the future of her own children are assured.'

'I admit I hadn't thought of that,' agreed the mother, giving in.

So, from that day until this the wedding day, all the arrangements had been in the Badyen's hands.

There was an outburst of cries, mingled with applause. A group of female griots was clustered around a woman who was handing out money.

'It's the best marriage of the year,' said one female griot. Bank-notes were pinned to her fulsome chest like decorations.

Her companion was enviously calculating her haul.

'I'm out of luck today. Everyone I meet seems to be broke,' she said.

'The day is not yet over,' the first said encouragingly, as she moved off towards another victim.

Above the heads and the head-dresses, in and out among the chanting griots, roamed the dishes of food: bowls of fritters, pails and plastic dishes full of ginger, flavoured with various kinds of herbs. In groups of six, seven, eight, or even as many as ten or twelve, people were regaling themselves with meat and rice.

The men who had united the couple at the mosque in their absence – the 'marriers' – now made their entrance. There were ten or more of them, all notables, in ceremonial dress. The Badyen welcomed them and made sure they were given comfortable seats. Then they were served liberally with refreshments – kola nuts, dishes of food and for each of them a large packet of fritters.

'*Alhamdoulillah*!' exclaimed one of their number, who seemed to be the spiritual leader of the community. 'Yalla's will has been done. These two people have been united before Yalla.'

'Which is something we don't often see these days in this country,' pronounced his neighbour sententiously.

Isolated from the other guests the elders discussed the present times.

The young people, who had attended the ceremony dressed in European clothes, were in another, smaller room, anxious to escape.

'The marriage is over. What are we waiting for now?' complained a bridesmaid seated near the door.

'It's stifling in here! It's time we went,' grumbled a young man adjusting his black bow-tie.

'What about some records?'

'I told you before, there's to be a band.'

'And what about the bride? Where has she got to?'

'She's at her mother's house with the marabouts, for the gree-grees.'

All together they began drumming on the walls, whistling and shouting.

At last when there was no more advice to be given and there were no more prayers to be said for a happy married life, N'Gone, in her white crêpe de Chine wedding dress, with its crown and white veil, was handed over by her parents, the Badyen and the elders to her escort of young people. As if from a single pair of lungs there rose a great cry. The Badyen's joy knew no bounds. She intoned the praises of the family lineage, backed by the female griots, who took up the chorus. Expensive cloths were laid in a carpet of honour from the bedroom to the front door. The bride and her large escort made their way along it.

In the street fifteen or so cars were waiting. At the rear, on a trailer, a two-seater car with a white ribbon tied in a bow like an Easter egg symbolized the 'wedding gift'. The horns sounding a mechanical serenade, the cortège set off through the streets of Dakar. People clapped and called out their good wishes to the bride as the cars passed by, with the trailer and its two-seater car following on behind like a trophy.

*　　*　　*

The villas were named after the wives. The first wife's villa, 'Adja Awa Astou', was situated on the eastern periphery of the residential suburb. Flame trees lined its tarred roads. A calm reminiscent of the first morning of creation pervaded this part of the town, where the officers of the peace patrolled in pairs without any sense of urgency. A well kept bougainvillæa hedge surrounded the house, and the wrought-iron front door bore an enamel plaque inscribed with the words 'Villa Adja Awa Astou'. The doorbell had the muffled tones of an oriental gong.

The first wife and her two eldest children were waiting in the over-furnished sitting-room. In spite of her age – she was between thirty-six and forty – and in spite of having borne six children, Adja Awa Astou had kept her slim figure. Her colouring was a soft black; she had a prominent forehead above the delicate line of her nose which flattened very slightly at the sides; her face was alive with subdued smiles and there was frankness in her almond-shaped eyes. There emanated from this deceptively fragile woman great strength of will and determination. Since her return from the Holy Place she dressed only in white. She had been born on the island of Gorée and had given up her Christian faith so as to enjoy more fully the pleasures of married life. At the time of their marriage, El Hadji Abdou Kader Beye was still a primary-school teacher.

11

Speaking in a restrained voice, with an intense gleam in her eyes, Adja Awa Astou repeated what she had said a few moments before:

'My co-wife and I should attend the ceremony. It's your father's wish. So . . . '

'Mother you can't expect Mactar and me to believe that you are happy about this third marriage and that it is taking place with your agreement.'

Rama, her eldest daughter, with her face thrust forward and her short hair plaited, was consumed with anger and reproach.

'You are young still. Your day will come if it pleases Yalla. Then you will understand.'

'Mother, I am not a child. I'm twenty. I will never share my husband with another woman. I'd rather divorce him.'

There was a long silence.

Mactar, who admired his elder sister, looked away out of the window into the distance beyond the flowers. He avoided his mother's eyes. The sharp pangs he felt in his heart grew worse. In spite of her directness, Rama was anxious to be tactful. She had grown up during the upheavals of the struggle for Independence, when her father and others like him had fought for freedom for everyone. She had taken part in street battles and pasted up posters at night. With the evolution of African society she had joined political associations, been a university student and a member of the Wolof language group. This third marriage of her father's had taken her by surprise and deeply disappointed her.

'It's easy to talk about divorce, Rama,' her mother began slowly. What she was about to say was the product of much careful reflection. 'You think I should get a divorce. Where would I go at my age? Where would I find another husband? A man of my own age and still a bachelor? If I left your father and with luck and Yalla's help found a husband, I would be his third or his fourth wife. And what would become of you?'

As she finished speaking, she smiled, just a little, to soften the impact of her words. Had she convinced Rama? She did not ask herself this question. Adja Awa Astou kept no secrets from her children.

Angry with impotence, Rama rounded on her mother:

'Don't you realize, mother, that this villa belongs to you? Everything in it is yours. Father owns nothing here.'

12

'Rama, I know that too. But it was your father who gave it to me. I cannot turn him out.'

'I won't go to this wedding.'

'I will. I must put in an appearance. If I don't it will be said that I am jealous.'

'Mother, that wife of my father's, that N'Gone, is my age. She's just a whore. You are only going because you're afraid of what people will say.'

'Don't talk like that!' her mother interrupted her. 'It's true N'Gone is your age. But she's only a victim. . . .'

The gong gave its oriental sound.

'It's your father.'

El Hadji Abdou Kader Beye came into the sitting-room with a sprightly step.

'Greetings!' he said to the two children. 'Are you ready?' he asked his wife.

'Yes.'

'And you, Rama?'

'I'm not going, father.'

'Why not?'

'Father, can you give me some money for school?' asked Mactar, approaching his father. El Hadji took out a bundle of notes and counting five gave them to his son.

Rama stood where she was. She caught her mother's eye and said:

'I'm against this marriage, father. A polygamist is never frank.'

El Hadji's slap struck her on her right cheek. She stumbled and fell. He moved towards Rama to repeat the blow. Quickly Mactar stepped between them.

'You can be a revolutionary at the university or in the street but not in my house. Never!'

'This is not your house. Nothing here belongs to you,' retorted Rama. A trickle of blood ran from the corner of her mouth.

'Come, El Hadji. Let us go,' said the girl's mother, pulling her husband towards the door.

'You should have brought that child up properly,' El Hadji shouted at his wife.

'You are right. Come, they are waiting. It's your wedding day.'

When their parents had left, Mactar ventured:

13

'Father is becoming more and more reactionary.'

Rama got up and went to her room.

As the Mercedes drove slowly away the man and his first wife sat silent, looking in opposite directions, anxious.

The second wife's villa was identical with the first's except for the hedge. Trees provided shade at the front. The front door had an enamel plaque with the words 'Villa Oumi N'Doye' in black lettering.

Modu the chauffeur drew up at the entrance and opened the door of his employer's car. El Hadji Abdou Kader Beye climbed out and stood for a moment on the pavement. Then he put his head through the window and said to Adja Awa Astou:

'Come on, get out!'

Adja Awa Astou glanced at her husband and shook her head. Her eyes were lifeless, they had a deep inscrutability that seemed like a total absence of reaction. But there was the strength of controlled inertia burning in them.

El Hadji could not sustain her look. He turned away. Then, as if he were addressing someone else, he pleaded with her:

'Adja, either you get out or you return home. What will Oumi N'Doye think?'

Adja Awa Astou had not lowered her eyes. Etiquette? She struggled to keep her temper. Deep inside her like an angry sea, her resentment welled up. But since she was sincerely religious she controlled herself and tamed her fury, imploring Yalla to help her. Restraining the urge to speak out, she said:

'El Hadji, I beg you to forgive me. You seem to forget that I am your Awa*. I will not set foot in that house. I'll wait here.'

El Hadji Abdou Kader Beye knew his first wife's pride very well. As soon as she finished speaking her bearing became rigid again and she turned her face away from him. Her husband crossed the garden and pushed open the front door of the villa. He entered the sitting-room, full of expensive French furniture and artificial flowers. As soon as he appeared the youngest daughter, Mariem, flung her arms

* 'Awa' is the Arabic name for the first woman on earth and the title given to the first wife.

14

joyfully round his neck. She was fifteen years old, big for her age, and wore a mini-skirt.

'Shouldn't you be at school?' asked her father.

'No, I've got permission to stay away today. I'm coming to the wedding with some of my friends from school. Father, can you give me some money?'

'All right. Where's your mother?'

Mischievously Mariem indicated where she was with her thumb. Her father gave her three bank-notes as he crossed the room.

Oumi N'Doye saw El Hadji in her mirror. She was securing her black wig with the aid of pins.

'I'll be with you in a minute,' she said in French.

'Who's with you in the Mercedes?'

'Adja Awa. She's waiting in the car.'

'Why doesn't she come in?' asked Oumi N'Doye immediately, turning towards the man. 'Mariem! Mariem!' she called.

Mariem arrived and stood with her hand on the door-knob.

'Mother?'

'Tell Adja Awa to come inside. She's in the car. Tell her I'm having my shower.'

Mariem went out.

'Is she angry?'

'Who?' asked El Hadji, sitting on the bed.

'Adja Awa Astou.'

'Not that I know of,' he replied, leafing through a woman's magazine.

'She persuaded you to marry this third wife purely out of jealousy. Just because I'm younger than she is, the old cow.'

Had her shaft gone home? El Hadji did not react. She had spoken with heavy sarcasm, gritting her teeth. There was still no reply so she went on:

'She's playing games now, your old woman. She's waiting outside just to see how I will take it, isn't she? Your old piece of dried fish-skin thinks I'm her rival. I bet you she'll gang up with that N'Gone to annoy me. But we'll see about that.'

'Listen, Oumi, I don't want any quarrelling, here or at the wedding. If you don't want to come that's your affair. But please stop talking like that.'

'What was I saying then? Now you're threatening me. If you don't want me at the wedding say so. That's what she said, didn't she? Your third, N'Gone, is no different from us.'

She stood facing the man, menace in her voice.

'Believe me, I'm not going to your third's to pick a fight. You needn't worry.'

'Get me something to drink. I'm very thirsty,' said El Hadji to change the subject.

'There is no mineral water in the house.' (El Hadji only drank mineral water.) 'Will you have tap water?' asked Oumi N'Doye in a mocking tone of voice and with an air of defiance that wrinkled the corners of her mouth.

El Hadji Abdou Kader Beye left the room. Outside he called his chauffeur Modu.

'Sir?'

'Bring me some mineral water.'

Beside the Mercedes Mariem was trying her best to cajole Adja Awa Astou from the car into the house.

'Mariem, tell your mother I'd rather wait here.'

'Mother Adja, you know how long my mother takes to get ready. She's having a shower,' said the child.

Defeated by Adja Awa Astou's smile Mariem returned in dejection to the house, followed by Modu carrying the portable ice-hamper.

As they came out of the front door Oumi N'Doye whispered to El Hadji:

'Which of us is to sit in the back with you?'

Before El Hadji could reply she continued: 'All three of us then. After all it isn't her *moomé*.'*

Settling herself in the Mercedes Oumi N'Doye asked after the health of her co-wife's children. The conversation between the two women was distant and full of courtesy. Each complimented the other on her clothes.

'So you don't want to come into my house?'

'You mustn't misunderstand me. I was comfortable in the car. I

* *Moomé*, or *ayé*, is the period a polygamist spends with each of his wives in turn.

don't get out because I still have those attacks of dizziness,' said Adja Awa Astou by way of apology.

El Hadji Abdou Kader Beye, seated in the back between his two wives, let his mind wander, only half listening to what they were saying.

They could hear the band – playing modern music – from some way off. A crowd of youngsters were dancing among themselves on the pavement. Stewards stood guard on the entrance, examining the guests' invitations before letting them in. Couples were dancing on the cement floor of the courtyard. Under the verandah a *kora*-player with two women accompanists took advantage of breaks in the band's playing to show what he could do, singing at the top of his voice.

The third wife's villa, which was of recent construction, stood outside the more heavily populated residential area in a new suburb intended for people of means.

The Mercedes pulled up.

Walking two paces ahead of his wives El Hadji crossed the courtyard amid the acclamations of the guests and the frenzied playing of the band, which completely drowned the efforts of the *kora*-player.

Yay Bineta reached the wives before the bride and in her role of mistress of the house she welcomed them and escorted them to a room where all the most distinguished women guests were congregated. Urbane as ever the Badyen abounded in civilities towards the co-wives.

'You will give a good example to the young ones, won't you? Good co-wives should be united.'

'Don't worry, we are used to it. We are one family. The same blood flows in our children's veins,' parried Oumi N'Doye, not giving Adja Awa Astou a chance to say anything. 'I take Adja our senior as my example. I thank Yalla for putting me to the test so that in my turn I too can show that I am not jealous or selfish.'

'Your presence here today speaks in your favour. All N'Dakaru knows you both. Your reputations are well established.'

The co-wives and Yay Bineta knew they were only playing to the gallery. They resorted to euphemism in preparation for the real hostilities which would come later. The Badyen left them and went to look for El Hadji in the bridal chamber. The room was decorated completely in white. A mattress laid on the floor in a corner, an upside-down mortar and a woodcutter's axe-handle were for the moment the only furnishings.

18

'It is time for you to change, El Hadji,' the Badyen told the man.

'Change? What for?'

'You must put on a caftan without trousers and sit there on the mortar, with the axe-handle held between your feet, until your wife's arrival is announced.'

'Yay Bineta, you don't really believe in all that! I have two wives already and I did not make a fool of myself with this hocus-pocus on their account. And I am not going to start today!'

'You're not a European, although I can't help wondering. Your two wives are somehow too nice today; it troubles me. My little N'Gone is still innocent. She isn't old enough to cope with rivalry. Go and take your trousers off and sit down! I'll come back and tell you when your wife arrives.'

Being ordered about by a woman was not in the least to El Hadji's liking and he was sufficiently Westernized not to have any faith in all this superstition.

'No!' he replied curtly and walked out, leaving the Badyen standing by herself.

Adja Awa Astou and Oumi N'Doye had realized what the Badyen's game was when she had led their husband away. The same thought had occurred to both of them. Oumi N'Doye's courage abandoned her and she spoke what was on her mind:

'What are we doing here in this house?'

Because of the noise Adja Awa Astou leaned over towards her. 'What did you say?'

Oumi N'Doye looked around to make sure that no one was listening or watching them.

'What are we doing here, you and I?'

'We are waiting for our *weje** to arrive,' replied Adja, her eyes fixed on the base of the second wife's neck.

'Are you, the *awa*, going to do nothing? You must be in favour of this third marriage then. You gave El Hadji your blessing, didn't you?'

Oumi N'Doye stuck out her chin. The light from the doorway lit up her face animated by jealousy. She pursed her lips.

'You want us to leave?' asked Adja confidentially.

'Yes, let's get away from here,' replied Oumi N'Doye, making to rise to her feet.

* *Weje* means co-wife.

Adja Awa Astou held her by the knee, as if to rivet her to her seat. Oumi N'Doye followed her eyes. Standing in the doorway opposite Yay Bineta was watching them. Intuition told the Badyen that the co-wives were discussing her goddaughter. She moved off.

After a moment Adja Awa Astou went on:

'It is Yay Bineta who is your rival. I have never entered the fray. I am incapable of fighting or rivalry. You know that yourself. When you were a young bride you never knew I existed. I have been the *awa* for nearly twenty years now, and how many years have you been his wife, my second?'

'Seventeen years, I think.'

'Do you know how many times we have met?'

'To tell the truth I don't,' admitted Oumi N'Doye.

'Seven times! During the fifteen or so years you have been the second wife that man, the same man, has left me every three days to spend three nights with you, going from your bedroom to mine. Have you ever thought about it?'

'No,' said Oumi N'Doye.

'And you have never been to see me!'

'Yet you have come to see me several times. I really don't know why I have never visited you.'

'Because you regarded me as your rival.'

The Badyen interrupted them. 'You have eaten nothing! Come on, help yourselves. You must act as if you were at home.' She placed a tray of drinks beside them.

Adja Awa Astou drank. Before raising the glass to her mouth Oumi N'Doye dipped her little finger into the liquid and scattered a few drops on the floor. Scandalized, Yay Bineta hurried off.

'The bride! The bride!'

The rest of the sentence was drowned in the general uproar that followed. A fanfare of car horns reverberated through the air. A thick-set woman with a shoe in her hand rushed towards the door. She was knocked over and fell to the floor. Her tight-fitting dress split, a long, horizontal tear which exposed her behind. She was helped back to her feet by a couple of women and roundly abused the male guests for their lack of manners and consideration for women.

Yay Bineta, the Badyen, pushed the crowd aside. In keeping with

21

their usual exhibitionism the President of the 'Businessmen's Group' led El Hadji forward to meet his bride.

El Hadji Abdou Kader Beye's head had been covered in a cloth.

The two co-wives went to the top of the stairs. From this vantage point they followed the enthronement. They too, at the start of their own marriages, had lived that moment, their hearts full of promise and joy. As they watched someone else's happiness the memory of their own weddings left a nasty taste. Eaten up with a painful bitterness they shared a common sense of abandonment and loneliness. Neither spoke.

Already El Hadji was on the dance-floor with his bride, inaugurating the festivities that were to last all night. The band played the inevitable *Comparsita*. After the tango came a rock-'n'-roll number and the young people invaded the floor.

Things had got off to a good start.

Twelve men, each carrying a spit-roasted lamb, made their entrance. In their enthusiasm some guests beat the furniture with any object they could lay their hands on, while others simply applauded.

Adja Awa Astou hid her chagrin with a show of forced laughter.

'Oumi,' she called softly, 'I am going to slip away.'

'Stay a little longer. . . . Don't leave me alone.'

'I've left the children by themselves at the villa.'

Adja shook her co-wife's hand and went down the stairs. She walked along the edge of the dance floor and reached the street, which was lined with parked cars.

'Take me home.'

Back at the villa Adja Awa Astou felt unwell. She hid it from her children as they assailed her with questions about the festivities. She had thought jealousy was banished from her heart. When long ago her husband had taken a second wife, she had hidden her unhappiness. The suffering had been less then, for that was the year when she had made the pilgrimage to Mecca. She was completely absorbed in her new religion. Now that she was an *adja*, she wanted to keep her heart pure, free of any hatred or meanness towards others. By an act of will she had overcome all her feelings of resentment towards the second wife. Her ambition was to be a wife according to the teachings of Islam by observing the five daily prayers and showing her husband complete obedience. Her religion and the education of her children

23

became the mainstays of her life. The few friends she still kept and her husband's friends all spoke of her as an exemplary wife.

When she had given the children their supper she took her beads and prayed fervently. She thought of her parents. She longed to see her father again. He was still alive and living on the island of Gorée. After her conversion to the Muslim faith she had gradually stopped seeing her family. Then when her mother died she had broken with them completely.

Her father, Papa John as the islanders called him, was an intransigent Christian, born into the third generation of African Catholicism. He attended Mass regularly with all his household and enjoyed a reputation for piety which had given him a certain ascendency over his colleagues. During the colonial period he had been a member of the municipal council for a number of years. When he discovered that his daughter was being courted by a Muslim from the mainland, he had decided to have it out with her. He had asked her to accompany him on his daily walk and together they had climbed the steep path up to the fort. Beneath them the angry, foam-covered sea battered the sides of the cliff.

'Renée,' he said.

'Father?'

'Is this Muslim going to marry you?'

Renée lowered her eyes. Papa John could see he would get no reply. He knew a lot about this Muslim and his trade-union activities. He had heard about his speeches at political meetings criticizing French colonialism and its allies the *assimilés*. He could not visualize this man as his son-in-law and suffered in anticipation at the thought that he might one day be associated with his family.

'Will you become a Muslim?'

This time his voice had hammered out the question firmly.

Renée was flirting with the teacher, who was something of a hero with the young generation; nothing more. She had certainly given no thought to the conflict of religions.

'Do you love him?'

Papa John had watched his daughter out of the corner of his eye as he waited for a reply. Deep down he had hoped it would be 'no'.

'Renée, answer me!'

*   *   *

24

Rama's arrival broke the thread of her memories.

'I thought you were asleep,' said Rama, sitting on a chair.

'Have you eaten?' asked her mother.

'Yes. Were there a lot of people at father's wedding?'

'With all that he spent on it! You know what the people of this town are like!'

'And Oumi N'Doye?'

'I left her there.'

'I suppose she was unpleasant.'

'No. We were together.'

Rama was sensitive to her mother's least suffering. The atmosphere did not encourage conversation. The light from the wall-lamp and the white scarf wound round her head made her mother's face look thin. Tiny bright dots shone in her eyes. Rama thought she could see tears on the edge of her lashes.

'I'm going to work for a bit before I go to bed,' announced Rama, getting to her feet.

'What have you got to do?'

'I have a Wolof translation to finish. Pass the night in peace, mother.'

'And you too.'

The door closed, leaving Adja Awa Astou alone again. As others isolate themselves with drugs she obtained her own daily dose from her religion.

*   *   *

Rock-'n'-roll alternated with the *Pachanga*. The dancers – only young people – did not bother to leave the dance-floor. The band put everything they had into their 'soul' music. The wedding had lost some of its solemnity and the guests were enjoying themselves.

The 'Businessmen's Group' sat apart. They were engaged in lively discussion, jumping from one subject to another, from politics to birth-control, from communism to capitalism. On their table were the different shaped bottles of every conceivable brand of alcohol and the remains of wedding-cake and roasted lamb.

El Hadji Abdou Kader Beye was being very sociable, flitting like a butterfly from group to group. The bride was dancing with a young man. Laughing, El Hadji joined his business colleagues.

'Are you leaving now? Off to deflower your virgin!' the President of the 'Group' greeted him with unsubtle innuendo. His breath smelt and he was unsteady on his feet. Putting his arm around El Hadji's neck he addressed the others in a thick voice: 'Friends, our brother El Hadji will be off in a moment to "pierce" his fair lady.'

'A delicate operation!' contributed the member of parliament, rising with difficulty from his seat. After a string of smelly burps he went on: 'Believe me, El Hadji, we'll gladly give you a hand.'

'Yes, indeed!' the others chimed in.

Each added his bit.

'Have you taken the "stuff", El Hadji?' asked Laye, joining them. He could not take his lecherous eyes off the prominent thighs of a girl doing the rock-'n'-roll. Whispering in El Hadji's ear, he said: 'I promise you, it works. Your *kiki* will be stiff all night. I brought the stuff back from Gambia for you.'

The conversation turned to the subject of aphrodisiacs. They all knew a great deal about them; each had his own favourite recipe. The young man escorted the bride back to her husband and N'Gone's arrival killed the discussion. Suddenly the lights went out. Cries of 'Oh!' and 'Lights!' and 'Give us our money back!' went up all round. When the lights came on again the bride and groom had disappeared.

In the nuptial chamber Yay Bineta, the ever busy Badyen, had finished her preparations. Now she had only to wait for the act in which it would all culminate. The bed was ready, with its white sheets.

'How happy I am, my children,' she said. 'The whole family was here – brothers, cousins, nephews, nieces, aunts and relations by marriage. It has been a great day for us all. You must be tired.'

'Me? No,' replied N'Gone.

'I'll help you to get ready,' said the Badyen to her goddaughter, all motherly. She began with the white crown, which she placed on the head of a tailor's dummy. She talked. 'Don't be afraid. You will feel a little pain but be docile in your husband's arms. Do what he says.'

Whether from modesty or shyness, N'Gone began crying.

El Hadji Abdou Kader Beye had gone into the bathroom. After his shower he swallowed a couple of pills to give himself strength. Hands in his pockets and smelling of cologne, he went back into the room. N'Gone, clad in a thin nightdress, was lying on the bed: the offering.

The Badyen had left. The man gazed at the girl's body with greedy insistence.

*   *   *

A light, nippy breeze was blowing on this side of the town. The muezzins could be heard calling the faithful to the *Facjaar* prayer. In the east, between the buildings and above the baobab and silk-cotton trees, the streaked horizon was growing lighter.

Slipping among the remaining shadows, an elderly woman, covered from head to foot, arrived at the door of the villa. The Badyen, who had been looking out for her for some time, let her in. They exchanged a few, brief words, then together they approached the couple's door.

Yay Bineta knocked. No reply. She knocked again. The two women exchanged glances. A vague anxiety appeared in their eyes. The Badyen turned the knob and slowly pushed the door open. She peered hesitantly inside. She was met by the blue light of the room. Frowning, she looked around.

N'Gone was in bed in her nightdress. At the foot of the bed sat El Hadji Abdou Kader Beye, hunched forward, his head in his hands.

Followed by the other woman carrying a cock, Yay Bineta entered the room. The Badyen examined the sheets for traces of blood. Then she placed the cock between N'Gone's things, ready to kill it in sacrifice.

'No! No!' N'Gone cried, closing her legs like a large pair of scissors. Sobbing, she tried to thrust the cock away from her.

'What has happened?' demanded the Badyen.

N'Gone's sobs faded into silence.

'El Hadji, I am talking to you. What has happened?'

'Yay Bineta, I did not manage it.'

N'Gone let out a cry, the cry of an animal in distress. The two women raised their hands to their mouths in astonishment. The cock escaped, crowing.

'*Lâa . . . lahâa illala!* Someone has cast a spell on you.'

The Badyen muttered to herself, while the other woman tried on all fours to catch the cock. The bird ran out of reach. The Badyen raged. 'I warned you this would happen. You and your like take yourselves for Europeans. If you had listened to me yesterday you would not be

27

in this situation now. The shame of it! What difference could it have made to you to sit on the mortar? (She pointed to it.) Now that you are as you are, what are you going to do about it? You must find a cure. You must see a marabout.'

The other woman cornered the bird behind the mortar and caught it by its legs. Nearby stood the tailor's dummy wearing the wedding-dress. She went up to El Hadji.

'The *xala** is nothing to worry about! What one hand has planted another can pull up. Get up! You have no need to feel ashamed.'

Xala! El Hadji Abdou Kader Beye was aghast. He could not believe what had happened to him. When he had talked about the *xala* to other men he had always treated it as a joke. This morning he was completely shattered. He felt numbed. He could barely realize what had happened. All night he had stayed awake, his body separated from his desire, his nerves disconnected from his nervous centre.

The Badyen went over to the bride.

'Stop crying now. You have nothing to blame yourself for. It's up to your husband to take the necessary precautions. I am sure you are a virgin.

Holding her cock tight the other woman admonished El Hadji. 'Pull yourself together, El Hadji! Get up! You must do something! Do something! You must find a cure.'

El Hadji went into the shower. While he was away, Yay Bineta hunted under the pillow for the licence and the keys of the wedding gift car. Having found what she was looking for, she proceeded to call the co-wives all the names she could lay her tongue to.

When El Hadji reappeared he was dressed.

Outside it was day. The courtyard was strewn with empty bottles, broken glasses, overturned tables and chairs. There were flies every-where.

Modu was waiting for his employer. When he saw him coming he threw away his cigarette. El Hadji's scowling face suggested to him something quite different from the truth – an exhausting night.

Installed in the Mercedes El Hadji Abdou Kader Beye did not know what he should do. He thought of going to see Adja Awa Astou. Twice he rejected that idea. What would he say to Asta? He could not order his thoughts. Which of his wives had planned it? Which of them
* Pronounced 'hala'.

had made him impotent? And why? Which of them? Adja Awa Astou? Unthinkable. She who never said anything out of place. It must be his second then, Oumi N'Doye. The *xala* could easily be her doing. She was very jealous. Ever since he had told her of his marriage *moomé* spent with her had been nights of hell. Yet in his heart of hearts El Hadji rejected that idea. Oumi N'Doye was not so spiteful. His thoughts kept returning to his wives.

Modu drew up in front of the import-export shop that was also his office. His secretary-saleslady, seeing her employer arrive, stopped her work with the Flytox and hurried forward to congratulate him.

'It was wonderful yesterday. My congratulations.'

'Thank you, Madame Diouf,' replied El Hadji, taking refuge in the tiny room he called his office.

Madame Diouf resumed her battle against the never-ending invasion of flies, cockroaches and geckos.

El Hadji Abdou Kader Beye was very depressed. He contemplated the door of his office, without seeing anything of the carpenter's bad handiwork. The noise from the street reached him, interrupting his reflections. The monotonous scraps of a beggar's chanting on the other side of the road got on his nerves. He returned to reality like a drowning man who reaches the surface and finds he can breathe again. To his surprise he found himself already regretting this third marriage. Should he get a divorce this very morning? He put that solution out of his mind. Did he love N'Gone? The question brought no clear answer. It would not upset him to leave her. Yet to drop her after all he had spent seemed intolerable. There was the car. And the villa. And all the other expenses. To repudiate her now would hurt his male pride. Even if he were to reach such a decision he would be incapable of carrying it out. What would people say? That he was not a man.

There had been a time when he had loved (or at least desired) N'Gone. She had attracted him. And now? What would become of him? What was he to do?

*　　*　　*

Modu sat on his stool, his back against the wall, as he supervised the little boy who was washing the car. His torso bare, the lad was busily wiping the car with a sponge. Modu was one of his best customers, for his employer was a man of importance. At the corner of the same crowded, busy street, on the right-hand side, the beggar sat cross-legged on his worn-out sheepskin, chanting. Now and again his piercing voice dominated the other noises. Beside him lay a heap of nickel and bronze coins, the gifts of passers-by.

Modu enjoyed the beggar's song. The chant rose in a spiral, up and up, then fell back to the ground to accompany the feet of the pedestrians. The beggar was part of the décor like the dirty walls and the ancient lorries delivering goods. He was well-known in the street. The only person who found him irritating was El Hadji, who had had him picked up by the police on several occasions. But he would always come back weeks later to his old place. He seemed attached to it.

*　　*　　*

Alassane, the chauffeur-domestic employed to drive El Hadji's children to and from school, was late this morning. He too had been celebrating the day before. He had a great weakness for beer. The morning round began as usual at Oumi N'Doye's villa.

As soon as Alassane hooted the children came running out of the house with their satchels.

'Alassane!' called Oumi N'Doye, still in her dressing-gown, from the doorway.

'Madam?'

'Have you seen the master this morning?'

'No, madam,' replied Alassane, helping the children into the vehicle.

'Alassane, when you have dropped the children, come straight back here.'

'Yes, madam,' he said, driving off.

Oumi N'Doye's offspring were in their places. The back of the mini-bus was divided in two. Each family had its bench. This segregation had not been the work of the parents but a spontaneous decision on the part of the children themselves.

*　　*　　*

30

In his office El Hadji Abdou Kader Beye was raging against the beggar. That vagabond! He had asked his secretary to telephone the President of the 'Group'. The wait seemed interminable. He ached between the shoulders. The telephone rang. He grabbed the receiver.

'Hullo! Yes! Speaking. I need your help, President. Yes, it's very urgent. Very. In my office. In an hour? Fine.'

He replaced the receiver and called out:

'Come in!'

It was Madame Diouf.

'Your second wife is on the phone. The other line.'

'Thank you. I'll take it.'

When his secretary had left the room, he picked up the receiver again.

'It's me. What is it Oumi? I had a lot to do this morning. I have my work to do. What? Come round to your place'. Now? I can't. What? Money? You've had enough already!'

El Hadji held the receiver away from his ear. At the other end Oumi N'Doye stormed:

'I'm not Adja Awa. After all you spent on this wedding, you can at least think of your children. I'm sending Alassane round.'

'A waste of time,' shouted El Hadji. 'I'll call this afternoon. Yes, I promise. Yes, yes!'

El Hadji nervously replaced the receiver and took out his hand-kerchief to wipe his damp face. Oumi N'Doye exasperated him. The woman was a spendthrift. Only the day before yesterday he had given her plenty of money. What had she done with it? His suspicions returned to her. Was she responsible for his *xala*? Why had she phoned him at the shop?

There was another knock at the door.

'Come in!'

It was the President, wearing a big smile.

'I thought you must be exhausted! So the "stuff" worked then?' he asked, settling himself comfortably into a worn-out easy-chair bought at a sale.

'It's not that,' said El Hadji, coming from behind the table. 'I have a problem. And you're the only person I can trust. I have the *xala*.'

The President started and looked up at El Hadji, who was standing over him.

31

'I'll be frank. I can't manage an erection with the girl. Yet when I left the shower I was stiff. Then when I got to her, nothing. Nothing at all.'

The President sat with his mouth open, unable to utter a sound.

The beggar's chant, almost as if it were inside the room, rose an octave.

'This morning the Badyen advised me to see a marabout.'

'You took no precautions?'

'What precautions? I've never believed in all that nonsense,' said El Hadji. The tone of his voice had changed, became agitated, as if broken. 'The Badyen wanted me to sit on a mortar.'

'When last did you make love?'

'The day before yesterday with my second wife.'

'Do you suspect anyone? Either of your wives?'

'Which one?' El Hadji wondered, walking over to the window and shutting it.

'These beggars should all be locked up for good!'

'Adja Awa Astou, for example?'

El Hadji turned round to face him. His face was expressionless, only his eyes moved.

'Adja Awa Astou?' he mused aloud. He could not make up his mind. He could not say for sure that she was responsible for his condition.

'No,' he confessed. 'Our sexual relations are very infrequent but she never complains.'

'The second then?'

Frowning, El Hadji pondered the possibility.

'Why would Oumi N'Doye do this to me? I spoil her more than the *awa*.'

'All the more reason for her to make you impotent. As long as she was the favourite she accepted polygamy and the rivalry. But now she has lost the privileges of being the youngest. She is not the first woman to behave like this and give her man the *xala*.'

El Hadji was impressed by the President's logic.

'You mean it is Oumi N'Doye?'

'No! No! I'm not accusing your second wife at all. But I do know that they are all capable of it.'

'I am a Muslim. I have the right to four wives. I have never deceived either of them on this point.'

33

The President realized his colleague was talking to himself.

'The thing to do is to go and see a marabout.'

'That is why I asked you to come round,' said El Hadji eagerly.

'I do know a marabout. But he is very expensive.'

'His price will be mine.'

'Let's go then.'

In the street the President said a few words to his chauffeur – a fat man with eyes reddened by chronic conjunctivitis who shook his head continuously – then took his place beside El Hadji in Modu's Mercedes.

*　*　*

At the same time as the President and El Hadji were driving in the Mercedes along the main road of the town towards the suburbs, Yay Bineta, the Badyen, was leaving the conjugal villa. She was in a mood of bitter disappointment. The man might be suffering physically from his *xala* but she was the moral victim. Her dreams had been shattered. 'I know how to defend myself. So El Hadji's wives want to get rid of us, do they? They want to humiliate us perhaps? I swear by my ancestors that within three months the co-wives will be repudiated and thrown away like worn-out rags. Or else they will kneel before my N'Gone like slaves,' she promised herself. She went past the two-seater wedding present, perched high on its trailer with its white bow. She had the key and the licence for the car under her cloth. She did not trust the man's intentions.

She crossed the road and hailed a taxi.

In order to understand this woman one needs to know her background. Yay Bineta had always been hounded by bad luck, *ay gaaf*. She had had two husbands, both now in their graves. The traditionalists held that she must have her fill of deaths: a third victim. So no man would marry her for fear of being this victim. This is a society in which very few women overcome this kind of reputation. She was seen as a devourer of men, the promise of an early death. Because of her *ay gaaf*, men kept out of her way, and married women of her age preferred to divorce rather than risk widowhood near her. Yay Bineta suffered deeply from her situation. She knew she was condemned to remain a widow for the rest of her life. In order to save face and to preserve the balance of her mind her parents had gone so far as to 'put her on offer', as it were. But no man would take it up.

The marriage of her brother's daughter was her marriage.

She exchanged the customary greetings and entered the single bed-sitting-room shared by her brother's children and grandchildren. Babacar was seated on a mat reading the Koran. Mam Fatou hurried forward eagerly to welcome the Badyen. She wanted news of her daughter. Had she really kept herself a virgin? Mam Fatou had not slept a wink all night.

'Can I talk?' asked the Badyen.

'Yes,' said N'Gone's mother, intrigued by the question.

'We have been insulted! El Hadji has not consummated the marriage.'

'What? What do you mean?'

Babacar stopped his reading.

'Just what I said. El Hadji has the *xala*.'

The three of them looked at one another without speaking.

'Babacar, did you hear?' said Mam Fatou breaking the silence.

The old man had been so taken by surprise he could only nod his head up and down.

'What's to be done?' asked Mam Fatou.

'El Hadji has gone to find a healer,' said Yay Bineta. 'His wives are bad, worse than whooping-cough in an adult.'

'To be honest I wasn't happy about this marriage from the start. It was too easy, too good to be true in these times,' said Mam Fatou, looking at her husband.

A heavy silence followed this remark.

'Say that again,' shouted the Badyen, ready to leap at her like a tigress. 'You should have said so before it was too late, and openly. El Hadji Abdou Kader Beye didn't force our hand.'

The Badyen spoke harshly and glared angrily at her sister-in-law, her face hard.

'You misunderstand me. I am worried for our N'Gone,' said the mother, anxious to avoid a quarrel with the Badyen.

Yay Bineta's dislike for her brother's wife was intense. She hated the woman for having turned her brother into a sheep.

'Babacar, you must go and see El Hadji and help him,' ordered Mam Fatou, addressing her husband.

'Where will I find him?' he asked.

'At his office. A woman can't talk to a man about such things,' said N'Gone's mother.

'She's right,' said Yay Bineta.

The old man closed his Koran, folded his mat in two and got to his feet.

'And the car?'

'It's outside their front door. Here are the keys and the licence. It's his wedding present, so the car belongs to N'Gone,' the Badyen explained.

Babacar went out, wearing his slippers. When they were left alone the two women put their heads together. They suppressed their mutual dislike in order to confront the ill-will of El Hadji's wives together.

*　　*　　*

An empty, cloudless sky. The torrid, stifling heat hung in the air. Clothes stuck to damp bodies. Everyone was returning to work after lunch, so the streets were very busy. Mopeds, bicycles and pedestrians streamed in the same direction towards the commercial centre of the city.

Old Babacar had returned home. He had waited all morning in vain for El Hadji Abdou Kader Beye. After *Tisbar*, the midday prayer, Mam Fatou had insisted he try again. 'He is your son-in-law after all,' she had told him. Walking close to the walls and the balconies he tried to protect himself from the sun's onslaught. He hoped he would find El Hadji.

The secretary-saleslady recognized him. She took him for a cadger come to collect his 'share' of the wedding. She told him to take a seat and returned to her work. She had three customers to see to. Others came after them.

The hours passed.

The old man listened to the beggar's chanting. He liked it. 'What a fine voice,' he thought.

The second wife, Oumi N'Doye, came in and without preamble spoke to the secretary bossily in French.

'Is he in?'

Madame Diouf looked up. A stray lock of her black wig hung

down over her narrow forehead. She recognized the newcomer. She pushed back the hair with her finger.

'No.'

'He left nothing for me?'

'No. But if you'd care to wait. . . This gentleman is also waiting.'

Oumi N'Doye sat on a chair, crossed her legs and opened the woman's magazine she had just bought. The secretary eased the fan towards her. Feeling the gusts of cool air the second wife thanked her with a sour smile.

Oumi N'Doye was a great expert on overseas women's fashions, those of the *grands couturiers* and the film stars. Photo-novelettes were her daily reading. She devoured them, believing everything in them, and dreamed of passionate love affairs she would have liked to experience. She had felt uneasy since the previous day. She found her husband's third marriage intolerable; it devalued her. The thought that she was a second choice, an option, enraged her. The middle position, giving her a kind of intermediate role, was unbearable for a co-wife. The first wife implied a conscious choice, she was an elect. The second wife was purely optional. The third? Someone to be prized. When it came to the *moomé*, the second wife was more like a door-hinge. She had given a lot of thought to her position in the man's marital cycle and she realized that she was in disgrace.

Oumi N'Doye could not overcome her feeling of ill-will towards Adja Awa Astou. 'Why doesn't she show disapproval of this marriage? She must be pleased about it, the old monkey-skin,' she muttered to herself. She, Oumi N'Doye, had been El Hadji's favourite. There had been times when she had kept the man longer than the code of polygamy allowed. There had been times too, at the height of her reign as the favourite, when she had robbed Adja Awa Astou of whole days and nights. The first wife had never complained, never demanded what was her right. Oumi N'Doye had come to think of herself as the only wife. Without the least concern for Adja Awa Astou she had accompanied El Hadji to receptions, even when it was not her *moomé*. With Adja Awa Astou she could accept the life of polygamy, but the advent of a third wife reopened the wound of frustration suffered by all the Muslim women of our country. She even thought momentarily of divorcing El Hadji.

'But why divorce him? Without a man's help a woman has to fall

38

back on prostitution to live and bring up her children. This is the way our country wants it. It is the lot of all our women,' her mother had told her, to persuade her not to divorce her husband. 'If you had a job one could understand your rejection of this third wife. Your first co-wife was a Catholic. How can you, born a Muslim, dare refuse? What is more your husband has the means to support you. Look around you. . . .'

Chastened by this advice Oumi N'Doye did not return to her parents with her complaints. She was not going to accept being forgotten, a woman who only saw her man to couple with him.

The telephone rang.

'Hullo! Yes. . . No,' said the secretary. 'I'll make a note. I don't know when the boss will be back. All right. Yes! Yes!'

Madame Diouf put down the receiver and looked at her watch.

'I have to close now. It is time,' she said, addressing Oumi N'Doye, who had got up.

'Where is El Hadji?' she asked.

'I don't know. He went out this morning with the President.'

Babacar had risen and stood at a distance.

'Young woman, I am the father of N'Gone, his third. When you see him tell him I'll expect him at my house.'

Oumi N'Doye stalked out in fury, without so much as a 'good-bye.' Her eyes had encountered Babacar's. She had given him a look full of animosity and the old man, unsure of its intention, had felt awkward. He followed the retreating woman with his eyes.

'Who is that?'

'It is El Hadji's second wife.'

'*La illaxa illa la*! I should have liked to make her acquaintance,' said the old man hurrying after her.

The shops and offices were closing. People were streaming back to the Medina and the dormitory blocks of the suburbs.

Babacar looked up and down the road. He saw her in the distance disappearing into a taxi. Then his attention was caught by the beggar. He dropped a coin onto his sheepskin and walked on.

Alassane had dropped Adja Awa Astou's children and was helping the other children out of the vehicle in front of Oumi N'Doye's villa.

'Alassane! Alassane! Wait a moment!' she shouted to the chauffeur.

She paid the taxi-driver and called out to her daughter. 'Mariem! Mariem! Listen! Come here!'

The child went up to her.

'Go and fetch your father for me. He is at his third's house. Tell him I must see him.'

'Mother, can I wash first?'

'Do as I tell you. Alassane, drive her there.'

'Yes, madam.'

Alassane drove off with the girl.

Back in the sitting-room Oumi N'Doye turned on the radio. She only listened to the international service, because the broadcasts were exclusively in French. She asked the maid if the master had come while she was out. No, he hadn't.

Mariem was back already.

'Father isn't there. No one has seen him all day.'

'Did you leave my message?'

'Yes,' said her daughter, helping herself to something to eat. The maid had laid out bread and butter, jam and dry cakes for the children's tea.

Mactar lay on the sofa with his legs in the air, in the throes of a fit of coughing. His mother shook the silver bell. The maid came.

'Bring Mactar a glass of water.'

'He eats too quickly, he's so greedy,' said Mariem, busily finishing her piece of bread.

The maid returned with a glass of water, which she gave to the boy. He drank.

'Sip it,' admonished his mother affectionately.

Mactar began to breathe more easily as his lungs filled with air. He gave a sigh of relief and wiped the unintended tears from his eyes.

'What were you going to say?' asked Oumi N'Doye in a motherly voice.

'Father should buy us a car. They have one at Adja Awa Astou's and father's third has one. While we. . .'

'His lordship has seen Rama with her Fiat, so he thinks that as the eldest he is entitled to a car as well,' said Mariem scornfully, picking up a magazine.

'Well, I'm a man.'

'And so what? Women also drive. It's mother who should have a car for her shopping.'

'Thank you, dear, for thinking of me. You're right, Mactar. I hadn't thought of it. All my money goes in taxis.'

Oumi N'Doye fell silent. The idea was a new one to her. She said to herself: 'There is a car at Adja Awa Astou's and also at the third's. And what do I have? Nothing!'

'I was the first to mention the car,' broke in Mactar.

'That's true, dear. I am going to talk to your father about it. Then you too will be able to go to school in your own car, instead of with all the others. You can run errands for me. Go round to Adja Awa Astou. If your father is there tell him I must see him. It is very urgent.'

'You promise to lend me the car?'

'I promise.'

Satisfied, Mactar ran out.

*　　*　　*

He did not find their father either. Oumi N'Doye was beginning to worry. El Hadji Abdou Kader Beye had assured her he would be coming. Usually he kept his promises. He was beginning to neglect her. After the meal, which she took alone with the children, she went to her bedroom with her magazines, still hoping. She got herself ready, making herself attractive. She was counting on keeping the man for a good part of the night. She lay on the bed looking very desirable and listened for his arrival. She turned off the main light, leaving a night-light, which seemed more appropriate. Nothing. She returned to her reading. Now and again she thought she heard the sound of a car-engine. It grew as the car approached then, to her intense disappointment, died away again. According to her alarm-clock it was nearly 1.00 a.m. She could not sleep. She felt threatened.

*　　*　　*

Late in the night El Hadji Abdou Kader Beye returned to his third's house. All was quiet and peaceful in the villa. A shaft of light shone from under the door. El Hadji knocked.

'Who is it?'

'It's me, El Hadji,' he replied, recognizing the voice of Yay Bineta, the Badyen.

She let him in.

'Have you passed the day in peace?' he asked.

'In peace only,' said the Badyen returning his greeting, and she added, 'N'Gone can't be asleep.'

El Hadji realized she was waiting for him.

'Have you eaten?'

'Yes.'

'If you are still hungry, your share is there. Have you done something about your problem?'

'Yes, I have seen a marabout.'

'*Alxam ndu lilay.*'

El Hadji went into the wedding chamber. Nothing had been changed. The bed was in its place, the tailor's dummy dressed. As on the night before, N'Gone was in her nightdress, ready. The night-light dimly lit the sculptural form of her slender body. The strong desire he felt for her faded away. As he had done the previous night, he tried desperately to excite himself mentally. Not a nerve in his body responded. He felt ill. He perspired. He, the stallion who usually flung himself on women, was like pulp. Regret and anger filled him. His body was taken over by bitterness. He felt the full extent of the seriousness of his predicament as a wounded male and was bewildered by it. He had dreamed of this moment as he lay in the arms of his other two wives, the moment when he would be alone with N'Gone. He had desired her with his whole body. He had carried his victim to the nest like a victorious bird of prey and now consummation seemed impossible, forbidden.

* * *

The *xala*, which had started off as a confidential matter to be discussed in whispers, had become, as the days then the weeks went by, a subject of general conversation.

El Hadji Abdou Kader Beye had consulted a host of *facc-katt* healers. Each had given his prescription. He had been anointed with *safara* – a liquid which the healer obtains by washing off verses of the Koran written on small planks of wood called *alluba* – and made to

42

drink it. He was given *xatim* (pronounced 'hatim'), esoteric writings, to wear round his waist like fetishes. He was rubbed with ointments. He was made to cut the throat of a completely red cock. He did everything he was told to do in the hope of a cure. When they saw the Mercedes draw up in front of their grass huts or hot, cast-iron houses and out of it climb a man in European dress, the *facc-katt* all knew their patient to be a man of substance. He was required to pay high fees, nice fat ones. He always paid cash.

Each of the experts gave lengthy explanations. Some said he was the victim of the jealousy of one of his wives. She was described to him: a woman of average build, perhaps small. He began to accept that it must be Oumi N'Doye. Another of the charlatans used and abused Yalla's name: his head was swathed in a thick turban and he pulled all the time at his forked beard; he had a bony face and wet sheep's eyes, and accompanied each sentence with an unctuous smile. Gazing all the time at a blackish liquid in a champagne bottle, he informed El Hadji that his *xala* was the work of a colleague who wished him harm.

El Hadji mentally reviewed the members of the 'Businessmen's Group'. It was a wasted effort.

The charlatan cleared his throat, making a strange noise as he did so, and returned to his contemplation of the bottle. No doubt at all, he could see the author of the *xala*: a well-built specimen, dark, but not excessively so.

Days and weeks passed. At his 'office' El Hadji Abdou Kader Beye would spend hours lost in thought, his mind far away. His eyes no longer followed his secretary-saleslady, Madame Diouf. Before, whenever she turned her back, he would ogle her nicely rounded buttocks, her well-shaped thighs. His secretary's behind was a great source of jokes and laughter among his friends.

El Hadji suffered greatly from his *xala*. His bitterness had become an inferiority complex in the company of his peers. He imagined himself the object of their looks and the subject of their conversation. He could not endure the asides, the way they laughed whenever he went past, the way they stared at him. His infirmity, temporary though it might be, made him incapable of communicating with his employees, his wives, his children and his business colleagues. When he could allow himself a few moments of escape he imagined himself a carefree child again. Remorse overwhelmed him like a tide of mud covering a paddyfield. He thought back over his third marriage in the vain hope of finding some explanation there. Had he been in love with N'Gone? Or was it simply old age urging him towards young flesh? Or was it because he was wealthy? Or because he was weak? Because he was a libertine and a sensualist? Was it that his married life with his two wives had been intolerable? He asked himself these questions but he was careful to avoid the truth.

He was held in the blinding grip of an intense hatred. He aged overnight. Two deep lines starting at the top of the nostrils curved around his mouth, widening as they did so. His chin broadened. The lack of sleep showed at the edge of his eyelids and bathed his eyes in a reddish lustre crossed by threads which according to the time of day or the place would take on the colour of stale palm-oil.

El Hadji Abdou Kader Beye had found in the President of the 'Businessmen's Group' a sympathetic listener who also spared himself no verbal effort. He had for El Hadji's *xala* a throaty voice with a sympathetic ring to it which in our country always indicates a desire to be helpful.

'We shall find a good marabout,' said the President, undaunted by their failure to do so.

'As a friend,' he made a list of all the healers he knew. El Hadji placed his confidence in him. He had given up the struggle and was constantly on the verge of tears. A dense cloud took possession of his thoughts. Everything seemed to shake unsteadily. A skein of questions unwound itself in an endless thread through his mind.

Before his wedding night El Hadji had obtained the agreement of his two wives for him to spend thirty nights with his third. Thirty nights of feasting, one could say. Now he would have to return to the regular *moomé*. Each wife to have her *aye*. Adja Awa Astou first. Yay Bineta had given it her blessing. 'Perhaps with this cycle of *moomé* you will find out who is responsible for the *xala*,' she said.

El Hadji returned with his shame to the unending rotation of the *moomé*. Adja Awa Astou was as self-effacing as the religious law required. Their chat did not extend beyond the hedge around the villa. The children had been well-behaved during his 'absence'. The wife was careful not to touch on the *xala*. Did she even know about it? Her husband said nothing on the subject either. The two nights that

44

followed were identical. No sexual relations. The man showed no inclination for them. Her *aye* over, Adja Awa Astou watched her husband leave her for his six nights elsewhere, with his other wives.

Adja Awa Astou had no friends. She was lonely, very lonely. If she wanted to confide in someone or pour out her troubles, there was not a soul to whom she could turn. In her isolation she thought of her father. She missed Papa John terribly. There was a time when she used to go every Friday after the main prayer of the day to the Catholic cemetery to visit her mother's grave. The caretaker had noticed the regularity of this woman, who was always dressed in the same way with her head covered in a white scarf. He watched her suspiciously from a distance. Was she mad? A former nun perhaps? Or a thief? Then one Sunday Papa John, whom he knew well, came to see him because the everlasting flowers had been removed.

'The lady in white put them over there behind the wall,' the caretaker told him, pointing them out to him.

'Renée,' muttered Papa John to himself. Then aloud: 'Does this lady come on Sunday mornings?'

'No, on Friday afternoons. Her chauffeur told me she was her mother.'

Papa John returned to his island. He would have liked to see his daughter, speak to her. One Friday in the month of Ramadan (the Muslim month of fasting) the caretaker waited for Adja as she was leaving and said to her:

'Madam, I don't see your father any more. I hope it is nothing serious?'

Adja Awa Astou looked at him with apprehension.

'Since when has my father not been coming?'

'I don't know the date, madam, but it's several Sundays.'

'Thank you,' she said, giving him a couple of coins.

She returned to her villa and told her eldest daughter, Rama, to go and find out how her grandfather was. Thus it was that Rama travelled between them, the bearer of their messages to one another.

Adja Awa Astou was too modest ever to speak to anyone about her

45

husband's *xala*. She grew closer to her daughter, who began to return home early to keep her mother company so that she would feel less alone.

One evening she went to her daughter's room with a great urge to get things off her chest.

'Mother! Sit down!' said Rama, putting aside her book. 'I don't see father around any more, you know.' Adja Awa Astou looked round at the objects hung on the walls. 'Your father is very busy at the moment,' replied her mother picking up a book. Holding the book in her hands gave her courage. But she still hesitated to speak. Good wife though she was, amenable, and an excellent mother, she could not hide her unhappiness. The question which had been on her mind for so long came tumbling out:

'What are people saying?'

Rama looked at her mother. She was embarrassed but choosing her words carefully she said slowly:

'They are talking about father's *xala*.'

Adja Awa Astou drew in her chin, her eyes fixed on the book. There was a long silence. 'So everyone knows about it,' she said, speaking to herself. Slowly she raised her head and looked at her daughter:

'What should I do?' she said, her voice full of entreaty.

Rama remained silent. Her own feelings were divided. She was deeply opposed to polygamy. She knew what it was that kept her mother in that state: it was for their sakes, the children's. She excused this weakness but was unable to say so.

*   *   *

Two or three days previously Rama had gone as usual to meet her fiancé, Pathé, at the hospital. Pathé had finished his studies in psychiatry a year earlier and was now practising. It was the end of the day. A male nurse went up to Pathé:

'Doctor, the registrar wants you. It's urgent.'

Pathé set off down the passage. At the entrance to the waiting-room he came face to face with El Hadji Abdou Kader Beye. The two men knew one another.

'Nothing serious, I hope?' inquired Pathé reacting in a purely professional manner.

46

'No, nothing,' El Hadji replied hastily. Then: 'Doctor, I don't see you at Adja's villa any more. I hope you haven't quarrelled with Rama.'

The doctor smiled. He looked so young his superiors all marvelled at his precocity.

'No, I've been busy.'

'That's a relief. We'll see you soon then.'

Pathé opened the registrar's door.

'Did you see him?' asked the registrar, tidying his table.

'Who?'

'El Hadji Abdou Kader Beye.'

'Yes. Has he made a donation to the hospital?'

'No such luck. He came about something quite different: his third wife.'

'Pregnant already?'

'Alas, no. You must be joking. He hasn't been able to manage an erection for nights now. He thinks someone has made him impotent, so he came for a pick-me-up. Those were his words.'

They laughed.

'It's purely psychological,' said Pathé.

'Perhaps. He was all right before his wedding night. But on the night itself he couldn't consummate the marriage. He is convinced that it's a *xala*. You know what that is?'

'I've heard of it.'

'Well then, you have a case of *xala*.'

'What can I do? It wasn't me he came to consult. If you think science is powerless. . .'

'Don't speak too quickly, Pathé. Science is never powerless. There are many fields still to be explored. Besides we are in Africa, where you can't explain or resolve everything in biochemical terms. Among our own people it's the irrational that holds sway. Why not see what you can find out about his visits to the marabouts.'

'I'm not very intimate with him. I see his daughter of course.'

'There you are! You have a foot in the camp. That's all, thank you. I'll see you tomorrow.'

Outside Pathé chewed over his anger. A host of ideas raged in his head. Should he talk to Rama?'

'Lovely man, I'm here, here for you, even though you're late,' she said to Pathé, who had changed into terylene trousers and an African shirt with short sleeves and embroidery round the neck.

'I'm sorry I'm late.'

'You'll have to pay a fine! You spoke in French.'

Pathé often forgot this rule of their language association. Members who spoke French had to pay a fine.

'What fine do you impose?'

'Later.'

Rama released the handbrake and drove off in a cloud of dust. She loved speed. At a pedestrian crossing she just missed someone and skidded towards the pavement. A policeman advanced on them. Very politely, he asked in French:

'Your driving licence please, madam.'

Rama glanced at Pathé, turned, all feminine, to the policeman and said in Wolof:

'My brother, excuse me, I cannot understand what you are saying.'

'You don't understand French?' he asked in Wolof.

'I don't understand French, my brother.'

'How did you get your driving licence then?'

Rama chanced a glance at Pathé. He avoided saying anything to prevent himself from laughing.

'Give me your licence,' ordered the policeman peremptorily in Wolof.

Rama hunted in her handbag and handed him her licence. Leaning forward the policeman examined Pathé's face and suddenly blurted out:

'Doctor! Doctor! Don't you recognize me? You attended my second wife. You looked after her very well.'

'Did I?' said Pathé modestly.

'I recognize you. I don't know how to thank you. My wife is completely better now.'

'You know, we get a lot of people at the hospital.'

Rama leaned over to Pathé and signed to him that he was breaking the rules of their language association.

'Is this your lady, doctor?' asked the policeman in French.

'No. . . a sister. I am going to examine her mother.'

Rama jabbed him in the side several times.

'I hope her husband will be able to correct her!'

'I hope so too,' agreed Pathé solemnly.

'Thank the doctor for being so kind as to go with you to attend to your sick mother. If it weren't for him I'd take away your driving licence. You may go,' said the policeman to Rama in Wolof.

The policeman was a good sort really. He halted a mini which was coming from the opposite direction and signalled Rama to pass. Once they were out of sight they roared with laughter.

They went to the Sumbejin.

The sun, pale as twilight at this time of the year, sent its ochre rays obliquely onto the sea. On the bar terrace a few customers were enjoying the occasional breeze.

'Why did you tell him all those lies?' asked Rama as she sat down. 'I thought you didn't understand French.'

'*Touché*, lovely man!'

They roared with laughter again.

The waiter, well trained at the hotel school, stood by them, erect and impassive. Rama ordered a coca-cola, Pathé a beer.

'Foreign, sir?'

'Local,' Pathé replied.

'Do you think we will get married one of these days?'

Caught off his guard by the question but aware of its connection with the incident, Pathé was too intrigued to say anything. Then:

'What's against it?'

'That's not an answer. I want to know, yes or no, whether you still intend marrying me.'

The waiter brought their order.

'My reply is yes.'

'You know I'm against polygamy.'

'What's eating you?'

'You know about my father's third marriage?'

'Yes.'

'Apart from the enormous expense, do you know the rest?'

'No,' replied the doctor, remembering what the registrar had told him less than two hours previously.

'My father spent a fortune on this wedding, not to mention the car he bought his Dulcinea on condition she was a virgin. A virgin! I'm sure she's as much a virgin as I am.'

She paused, drank her coca-cola.

Pathé, wary of the young girl's unpredictability, waited for what was to follow. With his right hand he chased away a bee buzzing around his glass. Rama leaned over to him and with her index finger signalled him to draw nearer. Her elbow was resting on the table, her forearm vertical and her hand dangling free.

'What's the matter?' asked Pathé.

She looked the doctor straight in the eyes.

'What's the matter? My father's *xala* is the matter,' she replied straightening herself.

'How did you find out?'

Hadn't she seen her father leaving the hospital? This confirmed what she had heard. Without taking her eyes off him, a narrow smile wrinkling the corners of her mouth into a look of mockery, she leaned over to him as before.

'Father came to see me and as I am a *facc-katt* he said to me: "Rama, my dear child, I am impotent".'

'How did you find out?'

'So you know about it too?'

Taken by surprise, Pathé could only splutter.

'I saw father leaving the hospital,' she said. 'The whole of Dakar knows about the wedding and they also know about this other business now.'

'It's true your father came to consult the registrar. But what does your mother say about it?'

'Lovely man, do you really have any intelligence? My mother? She's just an "antique". Didn't she accept the second wife?'

'And your father?'

She showed him the cheek he had struck.

'The last time I saw my father I received his hand here. Here. And it was on his wedding day.'

'A well deserved present!'

'You're intelligent, lovely man. For your punishment I want another coca-cola.'

Pathé called the waiter and ordered a second drink.

'It's on my mother's account that I feel so angry about it. She's eaten up with guilt. When we're married I'll do everything I can to see she gets a divorce and comes to live with us.'

A cool breeze laden with iodine blew in from the sea.

50

The *xala* was all they could talk about and Rama could only think of her mother.

'What should I do?' The mother's question shook like a bell in her head. Rama thought about her conversation with Pathé. Perhaps there was a medical solution for her father's condition. It seemed doubtful though. But she did not know the reason for her doubt. She would have liked to answer her mother encouragingly, for her sake, to give her a little hope. But what if it turned out not to be true? If an excess of kindness born of affection were to raise her hopes too high, like the yeast the dough, her disappointment would be all the greater and her sense of having been let down all the more painful.

She looked at her mother. The woman's eyes reflected her complete confusion. She passed the book from one hand to the other. Her palms were damp with sweat.

'There is nothing you can do, mother.'

Rama had chosen her words very carefully. She wanted to help her recover her calm.

'I can't even go out. People stare at me like. . .'

The rest of her words were drowned in a smothered sob.

'Did you cause this *xala*, mother?'

Was it that her heart had become cold and dry? Or was it an expression of sterile tenderness? Rama could not decide which it was. She kept her eyes on her mother. Adja Awa Astou's thin face lengthened towards her chin. The oblique slits of her eyes narrowed, silvery specks the size of pinheads shone in her left eye. Her lower lip trembled slackly for a moment. Then she said:

'I swear by Yalla that it is not me.'

'Why then? Do you feel you are to blame?'

'Simply because I am his wife, the *awa*. In such cases the first wife is always blamed.'

'You should have spoken to father about it during your *aye*.'

'I can't talk to him about such things.'

'Would you like me to talk to him?'

'You have no modesty!' exclaimed Adja Awa Astou, getting to her feet.

The book fell to the floor. She went on furiously:

51

'How can you talk about such things to your father?'

She left the room, banging the door behind her.

Rama stared at the closed door in astonishment.

*　　*　　*

El Hadji Abdou Kader Beye followed the marabouts' instructions: he drank their concoctions, rubbed himself with their ointments and wore their *xatim* round his waist. In spite of all this – or perhaps because of it – there was no sign of improvement. He went back to the psychiatric hospital. Without restraint he opened his heart to the registrar, his voice full of emotion. He wanted 'to go to bed' but his nerves betrayed him. Yet he carried out the treatment prescribed. The registrar made some notes and asked him to come again later. Day after day, night after night, his torment ate into his professional life. Like a waterlogged silk-cotton tree on the river bank he sank deeper into the mud. Because of his condition he avoided the company of his fellow businessmen, among whom transactions were made and sealed. He was weighed down by worry and lost his skill and his ability to do business. Imperceptibly his affairs began to go to pieces.

He had to maintain his high standard of living: three villas, several cars, his wives, children, servants and employees. Accustomed to settling everything by cheque, he continued to pay his accounts and his household expenses in this way. He went on spending. Soon his liabilities outstripped his credit.

Old Babacar, his father-in-law, knew a *seet-katt* – a seer – who lived in an outlying district.

They went there.

The Mercedes could not reach the seer's house. Nothing but sandy alleys. They clambered across the sand on foot. The houses were part wood, part brick, with roofs made of corrugated iron, canvas or cardboard, held in place by stones, steel bars, car axles and the rims of all kinds of wheels. Small children were playing barefoot with a football of their own concoction. On the slope opposite the wasteland a long line of women carrying basins and plastic buckets on their heads were returning from the communal tap on the other side of the shanty town, where the real town lay.

The *seet-katt* was a big fellow with an awkward manner. His skin was rough and wrinkled. He had brown eyes and unkempt hair and wore only a pair of shorts cut in the Turkish style. He led them to the enclosure where he held his consultations. A sack served as the door. On the inside of the enclosure the 'door' had been dyed red and animal teeth, cats' paws, birds' beaks, shrivelled skins and amulets had been sewn onto it. An assortment of bizarre-shaped animal horns lay in a circle around the sides of the enclosure. The ground was covered with fine, clean sand.

The *seet-katt* enjoyed a certain renown as a hermit mystic. His serious activities extended beyond the limits of his own neighbourhood. With a wave of a skinny arm he invited them to sit on a goatskin. Because of his European clothes El Hadji hesitated for a moment, then seated himself as best he could on the ground. Old Babacar sat cross-legged. The *seet-katt* spread a piece of bright red cloth between them and took some cowrie shells from a small bag. First he said some incantations, then with a sharp gesture threw the cowries. He quickly collected them up again with one hand. Holding himself stiffly erect he looked his clients up and down. Abruptly he held out his clenched fist. Slowly the ball of fingers at the end of his skinny arm opened, like a sea anemone.

Deferentially old Babacar pointed to El Hadji.

'Take these and breathe over them,' ordered the *seet-katt*, addressing them for the first time.

El Hadji held the cowries in the palm of his hand and murmured a few words. He breathed over the cowries and gave them back to the *seet-katt*. The latter closed his eyes, muttering to himself in concentration. Then with a gutteral roar he flung the cowries onto the piece of cloth.

Like a shower of sparks in the dark the buried, ghostly universe of his early childhood rose to the surface of El Hadji's memory and held him in its grip. A host of spirits, gnomes and jinns paraded through his subconscious.

The *seet-katt* counted the cowries. Once. Twice. A third time. What? He raised his tobacco-coloured eyes up to his client. He scrutinized him. El Hadji was suddenly afraid. Why did he stare at him like that? The diviner gathered up the cowries and threw them down once more.

'Strange,' he muttered.

No one spoke

Before throwing the cowries again the *seet-katt* took a cock's spur from a red cloth in which it was wrapped and put it with the other objects. His face clouded over. His gaze became more penetrating. Stiffness? Desire to impress? Ritual gesture? He changed his posture. He leaned forward then straightened himself again. A smile of satisfaction spread over his face.

'This *xala* is strange,' he announced.

A feeling of immense joy came over El Hadji. His whole being was filled with a warm, comforting euphoria. He looked happily at his father-in-law. Why had he never heard of this *seet-katt* before?

'Who caused this *xala*?' asked old Babacar.

The seer was lost in contemplation.

From the distance came the noise of children, from nearby the sound of music – someone was walking past the compound with a transistor radio.

'I can't see who it is. Is it a man? A woman? Very hard to say. But I see you very clearly. There you are, as clear as anything.'

'I want to be cured,' said El Hadji spontaneously.

He waited anxiously for the reply.

'I am not a *facc-katt* – a healer – but a *seet-katt*. My job is to "see".'

'Who has done this to me?' asked El Hadji.

His face had aged so much it had taken on the expression of a Baule mask.

'Who?' echoed the *seet-katt*.

The fingers held over the fan of cowries seemed to be plucking the strings of a guitar. The *seet-katt's* eyes, like his fingers, followed an invisible line. 'Who?' he repeated. 'The shape is indistinct. But I can definitely say it is someone close to you. This *xala* was carried out during the night.'

'Tell me who it is and I will give you anything you ask. I want to be cured! Become a man again! Tell me how much you want,' shouted El Hadji in anguish.

Suiting the action to the word, he took out his wallet.

'I only take what is my due,' replied the *seet-katt* self-righteously.

His eyes encountered El Hadji's and he added: 'Do you only want to know the name of the person who has made you impotent?'

'Yes, that is what I blew onto the cowries,' admitted El Hadji regretfully. 'But you can treat me, cure me! Cure me!' implored El Hadji, waving the bank-notes.

The *seet-katt* carefully collected his instruments together and folded the cloth, without paying them any attention. He was completely lacking in deference now.

'How much do we owe you?' asked old Babacar.

'Five hundred francs.'

El Hadji handed him a thousand-franc note. Since he had no change he made him a gift of the rest.

Outside the house El Hadji turned over in his mind the sentence: 'It is someone close to you.' Just as nature re-imposes its life on ruins with small tufts of grass, the ancestral atavism of fetishism was being re-awakened in El Hadji. Like a torrent, his suspicions carried along names, imprecise silhouettes, faces without shape. He felt himself surrounded by treachery and ill-will. After his visit to the *seet-katt* he became more reserved, more touchy. Fatigue added its weight to his depression. He was haunted by what the diviner had told him.

It was Oumi N'Doye's *moomé*. He put off the moment when he would have to go to her. He was certain in advance that he would not be able to accomplish his conjugal duty with her. He finally arrived as late as he could in the evening.

Oumi N'Doye had prepared her *aye* in a spirit of rivalry. A re-union meal. The menu culled from a French fashion magazine. She wanted to make him forget the last meal he had had with his first wife. The table was laid in the French way. There were various *hors d'œuvres* and veal cutlets. The Côtes de Provence rosé kept the bottle of French mineral water company in the ice-bucket; at the other end of the table a pyramid of apples and pears. Next to the soup tureen cheeses in their wrappings. The planning of the meal was part of the second wife's campaign to reconquer lost ground. To regain her husband's affections. One of her women friends, prodigal with advice, had that very day whispered in her ear:

'If she is to have her man's favour, a wife who is obliged to compete with others must aim at the male's two most vulnerable parts: his stomach and his genitals. She must make herself desirable by being feminine, with just a touch of modesty. In bed she must not hold back. If she does she will only find disappointment.'

Oumi N'Doye had plaited her hair over her forehead in the

55

Khassonke style. She had twisted a gold ring into the middle plait, which hung down to her neck. On each side of her head, starting above her ears, five branches opened out into a heart-shaped fan, each topped with a flat mother-of-pearl. A thin layer of antimony accentuated her black eyelashes and eyebrows.

She sat opposite her husband and chatted away, doing most of the talking. Now and again she rang the bell for the maid.

'I had given you up,' she said, laughing. 'Yet I am your wife too, aren't I? A little older than your N'Gone, I know. Still, side by side, we look like sisters,' she concluded happily, her eyelashes fluttering like a pair of butterflies about to take off. On the side of her face in the light, her eye had the polish of china clay.

El Hadji forced a smile. He was scarcely eating anything. He was not hungry. He felt as if the room was closing in on him.

'You're playing hard to get with me now, aren't you? You could have phoned me. Oh, it's not for me. I know my place. It's for the children. What if one of them fell ill? Touch wood! But you never know. Me? I know when it's my *aye*. I make no demands. A thought costs nothing. A thought gives pleasure.'

El Hadji Abdou Kader Beye was wrapped in his obsession. 'Why not her?'

Oumi N'Doye talked on. She had been lucky to get the meat. Veal cutlets from France. Native butchers don't know how to cut meat. Don't you agree? The greengrocer's avocado pears weren't ripe. Only good for the *toubabs* (whites). Aren't there a lot of *toubabs* around now?'

El Hadji got up from the table. He sat down in the armchair and stretched out his legs. Tilting his head backwards he undid his tie. The harsh light of the lamp in the corner exaggerated the signs of age on his face. His short hair glistened white, like linen.

'Of course, when you eat at two tables you have your preferences,' she flung out acidly, still at the table.

After a brief silence she resumed, her voice very gentle: 'You must realize that when I speak to you it's also for the children. You must treat us all fairly as the Koran says. Each household has a car except this one. Why?'

El Hadji was not listening. He was completely absorbed in his *xala*. His thoughts turned to Adja Awa Astou, and at this moment he felt grateful for his first wife's reticence. As if he were about to be caught red-handed performing some shameful act he dreaded the moment when he would have to go to bed with his second. His heart was beating fast. He would have liked to miss out Oumi N'Doye's *moomé*. He could then have spent the night somewhere else, far away from her. He knew in advance that the woman would move heaven and earth to bring him back to her house.

'Answer me!'

'I didn't hear. What were you saying?'

Hands on her hips, she looked down at her husband.

'No one is more deaf than he who doesn't want to hear. I repeat, my children must also have a car. Adja has one, your third has one. I don't mind being on the tandem but I won't be the spare wheel. You're giving my children a complex about it.'

'No need to shout. You'll wake them.'

'Admit that I am right. Everything for the others. Nothing for me or my children.'

'Pass me the mineral water.'

Her anger was only a flash in the pan. She brought him the bottle and a glass.

'Shall I run you a bath?' she asked.

She had just read this in one of her magazines. El Hadji could hardly believe his ears. He looked at her, agreeably surprised.

'Yes, thank you.'

She disappeared.

After his bath El Hadji climbed into bed. Soon she was ready too. The room was filled with her perfume. Slipping into bed beside him she unbuttoned his pyjamas. Her hand travelled up and down the man's body, familiar with its geography. The exploration became more feverish and she pressed herself against him.

El Hadji Abdou Kader Beye had to endure this torture. His back was running with perspiration. Physical contact with Oumi N'Doye used once to stimulate his desire. Now the hand that caressed him inflicted the sufferings of hell. He was wet all over. His nerves were dead. He lacked the simple, humble courage of everyday heroism to tear himself from this misery which burned him like red-hot coals. Unable to help himself, tears welled up from deep inside him.

Oumi N'Doye interpreted her husband's attitude as an indication of her fall from favour. She flew into a rage. Her highly coloured verbal repertoire, rich in innuendo, hit its mark, filling the man with resentment. She suffered as well.

'Your old Adja has worn you out. Or is it your N'Gone? You have to be a good rider and a young one to mount two mares at the same time, especially at a canter,' she said. She came to the end of her outburst and turned her back on him.

Eventually, feeling calmer, his mind a blank, El Hadji slept in fits and starts. Each time he woke he could hear the beggar's chant unwinding itself.

The following morning, shaved and in a fresh change of clothes, he was having his breakfast – after the children's departure for school – when Oumi N'Doye came and sat down beside him. Her eyes were dull as a result of her unsatisfied night. There was an awkward barrier between them. El Hadji, anxious to justify himself, tried to explain. He blamed an increase in business activity. To win her forgiveness for his conduct of the previous night he took out his wallet and at the sight of the wads of notes she melted.

'Don't expect me this afternoon.'

'Where will you have lunch?'

'With the President. We have to meet some *toubab* businessmen and spend the day together.'

As he spoke El Hadji looked away towards the door. This lie gave him a feeling of relief, like a soothing balm.

'Come home early then. It's a long time since we went to the cinema.'

'All right,' he agreed as he left her.

Modu had noticed his employer's decline: his voice, his reluctance to look you in the eyes, his heavy hesitant walk. El Hadji had always been like a grandfather to him. But since his marriage he had become different, distant. After dropping him Modu went and sat on his stool, listening to the beggar. The car-washer busied himself about the vehicle as he did every morning.

The hours passed.

Yay Bineta, the Badyen, arrived, accompanied by the woman with the cock. As soon as she was seated opposite El Hadji, she said:

'How are you these days?'

'Thanks to Yalla, well.'

'Well? Well?' she queried.

El Hadji hesitated to answer in front of a stranger.

'Don't you recognize her? Surely you do? You must have been thinking of something else that morning! She's the one who came for the "cloth of virginity" ceremony.'

For a brief moment hatred mingled with embarrassment flowed over El Hadji. The prerogatives of this Badyen woman were quite extraordinary.

'And your other wives?'

'The same.'

The Badyen opened her mouth. A reflex action. She glanced at her companion.

'*Yam*! A bad case!' she exclaimed.

Regret? Hostility? Still confused and undecided she held back. Her agile mind, used to this kind of situation, was hard at work. She was taking stock. There was a question she badly wanted to ask. She hesitated and looked towards the window, pretending to listen to the beggar. Then:

'Have you been with your other wives. . . to try?'

'Nothing.'

'Nothing,' she echoed. She frowned, catching the cock woman's eye.

A long pause.

The Badyen's fertile mind was busy: 'If the wives are not complaining it's because they have caused this *xala*. They aren't just jealous, they're a real danger to my N'Gone.'

An idea began to take shape in the pauses of her inner monologue. Her long experience made her inclined to doubt a man's word. 'Is he virile? Is he the father of his children? These days women will do anything for money. They aren't made of rags. How can I find out the truth? The full truth?'

Yay Bineta tactfully changed the subject.

'I have seen Babacar. You should go and see him. He knows a good *seet-katt*.'

'We have been to him.'

'Oh,' she said innocently, feigning surprise. There was a glint of malice in her eyes.

El Hadji Abdou Kader Beye was sure old Babacar must have told his wife and his sister about their visit to the *seet-katt*. Why did the woman harry him like this? 'It is someone close to you,' he repeated to himself. 'Could it be her?' That woman went too far. Was she out to run his life? Would he have to tell her all its intimate details?

'You must do something quickly, before it is too late. We are looking forward to our *moomé*.'

El Hadji understood the inference but did not pick up the threat it contained.

'You must not forget or neglect us,' the Badyen went on. 'A young wife needs her husband. Love is fed on the other's presence.'

The two women got to their feet. El Hadji told Modu to drive them home.

'You will come and see us this evening? Just a courtesy visit. Six days is a long time to wait.'

'Yes,' he promised, as Modu put the car into gear.

Why had she come to remind him of N'Gone's *moomé*? Wasn't he her husband? 'Do something before it is too late.' What did she mean? And that threatening tone of voice! The woman revolted him.

El Hadji Abdou Kader Beye's business was feeling the effects of his state. He had not replenished his stock since the day after his wedding. (It is perhaps worth pointing out that all these men who had given themselves the pompous title of 'businessmen' were nothing more than middlemen, a new kind of salesman. The old trading firms of the colonial period, adapting themselves to the new situation created by African Independence, supplied them with goods on a wholesale or semi-wholesale basis, which they then re-sold.)

The import-export shop which he referred to as his 'office' was situated in the centre of the commercial district. It was a large warehouse, which he rented from a Lebanese or a Syrian. At the height of his success it was crammed with sacks of rice from Siam, Cambodia, South Carolina and Brazil, and with domestic goods and foodstuffs imported from France, Holland, Belgium, Italy, Luxemburg, England and Morocco. Household utensils made of plastic, pewter and tin were heaped up to the ceiling. Delicacies, preserved tomatoes, pepper, milk and sacks of onions blended their odours with the smell of damp walls and obliged the secretary-saleslady to use up two cans of aerosol a week.

He had made a den for himself in a corner, calling it his 'office'. He had furnished it with metal cupboards that had slots labelled with the months and the years.

Madame Diouf came to tell him it was midday. Since the Badyen's departure, he had been turning things over in his mind. He did not have a lunch engagement. He wanted to be alone. He could relax when he was on his own. He went to 'his' restaurant, where he went for business lunches or when he took a girl out. The owner of the restaurant, a Frenchman, knew him well and welcomed him with obsequious courtesy, congratulating him on his marriage and offering him an aperitif. As he showed him to his table he said:

'Africa will always be ahead of Europe. You're lucky you can have as many wives as you need.'

It was a simple meal: a grill with a salad, rosé d'Anjou, cheese. After coffee he felt like a siesta. Where? At his third's? His second's? His first's, the only villa where he would get any rest? On second thoughts he would do better to go to a hotel.

Modu had gone home. He'd have to go on foot! It was very hot and he would meet people he knew on the way. He took a taxi instead.

'El Hadji!' said the manager, a Syrian, welcoming him with hands outstretched in the Muslim way. 'You can have the same room with air-conditioning. What name if "anyone" asks for you?'

This was where El Hadji always came when he wanted to relax.

'I'm alone today,' he replied, entering the lift.

'Sick?'

'No. I need to think.'

'Here you are at home.'

He turned on the air-conditioning and the room filled with cool air. He soon dozed off.

How long had he been asleep? He looked at his watch. Seven in the evening. 'All this time!' he said to himself. When he reached the entrance he found Modu waiting for him. His employer's behaviour puzzled him. Why does a man go and sleep in a hotel when he has three villas and three wives? If El Hadji had had a rendezvous with a girl he, Modu, would have known about it. Because of the gossip he knew about the *xala*. A good marabout lived near his village. Could he find a way to tell El Hadji about him?

'The "office" is closed, boss,' said Modu, so as to discover where to drive him.

They stood face to face. Modu, who was a down-to-earth sort of man, could see the distress in his employer's eyes, which were encircled by thin folds of skin, a sign of tiredness. They had the yellow colour of old African ivory. Modu stood aside and opened the car door. The Mercedes drove off towards the village of N'Gor.

When they reached the foot of the twin humps El Hadji told him to drive to the top. The car went up the circular track to the lighthouse.

El Hadji got out of the car and walked a little way along the path. He looked into the distance, his face grim, his shoulders sagging. Below him, like an enormous lake, shimmered the surface of the sea. The spray, like a net curtain being shaken by invisible fingers, folded and unfolded itself, catching the reflections of the light. The sea seethed and roared. Calmly he retraced his steps, skirting the caretaker's hut. He stopped again. In the distance, Dakar. From afar like this the buildings, roofs and treetops gave the impression that the town was carved out of a single, whitish mass of rock into an irregular lacework with touches of shadow. The fronts of the buildings were lit by the moon's rays and a row of winking luminous dots lined the main street.

Vultures were gliding above in the sky.

El Hadji had stopped for no particular reason. Modu, who had remained in the car, was suddenly alarmed. Was El Hadji going to commit suicide? The fear became so insistent that he approached his employer in order to watch him and intervene if he did try to jump.

The time passed.

The lights came on in the city. Above their heads the bright beam of the lighthouse came and went.

El Hadji turned to his driver and said;

'Take me to N'Gone.'

He had promised the Badyen he would call in the evening.

Some people were sitting on the lighted verandah. Did he know them? It was not important. The Badyen introduced them: a twelve-year-old boy and his nine-year-old sister. N'Gone's brother and sister, who had come to live with her. It was normal that N'Gone should take her turn in bringing them up. She must relieve her parents of these mouths to feed, explained Yay Bineta, not giving him a chance to say anything. She thanked the man in advance. Beneath a shower of compliments about his generosity, goodness and loyalty, he entered the bedroom. Still in its nuptial state the white bed, symbol of purity, was waiting to be marked. The tailor's dummy still stood there, wearing the wedding dress and the crown.

N'Gone sat across the bed, leaning on one arm, in an effort to relax the atmosphere.

'I have been hoping for your visit since the other day. How are your wives? And your children?'

This banal chatter, which had nothing elevated or subtle about it, made El Hadji realize that with N'Gone he had built on sand. Not that he himself had much in the way of fine, delicate, or witty conversation. In our country, this so-called 'gentry', imbued with their role as master – a role which began and ended with fitting out and mounting the female – sought no elevation, no delicacy in their relations with their partners. This lack of communication meant they were no better than stallions for breeding. El Hadji was as limited, short-sighted and unintelligent as any of his kind. Only his present situation prevented him from exchanging with N'Gone a flow of trite, empty conversation. The arrival of the Badyen with refreshments brought the bride's chatter to an end.

'I hope I am not disturbing you? El Hadji must be thirsty. A man is always thirsty when he returns home from work,' opined Yay Bineta, placing at their feet a tray with two glasses and a bottle of lemonade.

She told N'Gone to serve her husband. 'These days young women don't know their duty.'

N'Gone filled the glasses.

'Good luck, my dear,' she said in French.

'I must go,' said El Hadji after tasting the drink.

He was embarrassed by the heavy silence and by the Badyen. The atmosphere clung to him and hindered his movements.

'Already?' said N'Gone in astonishment, leaning more heavily on the man's shoulder.

'N'Gone, remember El Hadji's car,' said the Badyen to her in the bright tone of voice of the schemer. She was standing beside the tailor's dummy as there was no chair.

'I'd forgotten all about it, Badyen,' said N'Gone in French.

'I don't understand that jargon,' said Yay Bineta, bridling.

Then, still addressing N'Gone, she said: 'You will see, your husband will agree with me. Won't you, El Hadji?'

'Yes,' he acquiesced, not knowing what it was all about, but solely to win the woman's good grace and facilitate his speedy departure.

'What did I tell you? You are lucky to have such a good man for your husband.'

Yay Bineta paused for a moment as if she had lost the thread of her thought. She was watching the man.

'Now, there's the car. N'Gone can't drive yet. She will need a chauffeur. There are errands to be run. Also her brother and sister live with her now and their school is on the other side of the town. And it's far.'

'I want to learn to drive.'

'The chauffeur your husband hires will teach you to drive. Lots of young women drive,' said the Badyen, interrupting her. Then very maternal: 'El Hadji, you decide between us.'

'I'll take on a chauffeur tomorrow. You can learn with him.'

'I'd prefer a driving-school. It's more reliable.'

'You'll do as you are told! A wife must obey,' thundered the Badyen, before slipping quietly away.

When they were left alone N'Gone talked at length about the qualities of the different makes of cars.

El Hadji used to forget his other wives when he was with this girl who was now his wife. He used to like her manner, her childish, laughing behaviour. She broke the drab monotony of his life. At the same time she made him feel strangely exalted, as if he were enjoying a second youth. Before, on the rare occasions when he was left alone with her, he had found it difficult to contain his desire for her. Now that she was offered to him N'Gone seemed to be the embodiment of mental and physical torture. She clung to him, clumsily took the initiative, like someone who had learned her lesson badly. She panted, pushed him over on the bed and lay on him.

Carefully he struggled free, straightened his tie and got up from the bed. He looked down at N'Gone. 'I am finished,' he said from the

64

depths of his misery. It was like a blow that echoed and re-echoed in his head, rolling and unfolding towards a limitless shore.

'I must go. It is late,' he said, his voice heavy with unhappiness.

Disappointed, N'Gone doubled herself up on the bed, her head in her arms. Then with a movement of her hips, she flung herself back and opened her legs wide. She looked at the man defiantly, provocatively.

'I'll be back,' murmured El Hadji, avoiding her eyes and the invitation they contained.

N'Gone remained still, in the same position, her face set. There was a heavy silence. El Hadji just stood there for a moment, then left.

*   *   *

Oumi N'Doye had put on her best outfit for the cinema. She was gay, amusing, full of banter. They went to an exclusive cinema where the clientèle was mostly European. Oumi N'Doye spoke to the people she recognized – Africans. For her this outing meant that El Hadji was taking an interest in her again. She showed off her man to draw attention to the fact that she was not abandoned, not for the moment at least. So she was noticed.

As soon as the film started El Hadji Abdou Kader Beye settled back comfortably in his seat. The film did not interest him. His thoughts were elsewhere. He wished the evening could last indefinitely.

After the cinema Oumi N'Doye wanted to go dancing. It was such a long time since they had been to a night-club, she said. They went to 'their' club, the one they had frequented when his second enjoyed his favour, where El Hadji had 'his bottle' of whisky kept for him. The couples moved like shadows in the semi-darkness, keeping time to the rhythm of the Afro-American 'soul' music. Oumi N'Doye was happy and did not miss a single dance. She flaunted her femininity, hungry for the men's attention.

They returned home late, a little tipsy.

El Hadji thought she was tired out and would leave him in peace. He had his bath and got into bed first, turning out the light. Alone in the dark he would forget his *xala* and sleep.

When did she join him in bed? He was sound asleep when she woke him with her hand running over his body, caressing him greedily. He did not respond.

65

'What's the matter with you?'

El Hadji did not reply, ashamed in his dignity as a man. The woman's rapid, warm breath swept his face.

'Tell me what's the matter with you,' she whispered, holding the man's flabby penis.

'I'm not in form.'

'And yesterday?' she said fiercely. 'I'm not made of wood, as the French say. I warn you, I can go elsewhere.'

Threat? Blackmail? El Hadji knew that his second wife never 'missed' two nights in a row, that she was passionate and sexually insatiable. She dropped the man's limp penis and raged about her rights as a wife according to the laws of polygamy.

The next day. Thursday.

They were all together round the table, having breakfast. The children, who rarely saw their father, were making the most of it. The eldest, Mactar, returned to the subject of the car, backed by his mother. Oumi N'Doye rubbed in her son's demands with irritating remarks. 'There should be equality between the families and the children. Why don't we also have a car? Are my children illegitimate? Bastards?' Mariem, the younger, emboldened by what she heard, talked about clothes, claiming she went naked to school, that the mini-bus had torn her dresses.

(It is worth knowing something about the life led by urban polygamists. It could be called geographical polygamy, as opposed to rural polygamy, where all the wives and children live together in the same compound. In the town, since the families are scattered, the children have little contact with their father. Because of his way of life the father must go from house to house, villa to villa, and is only there in the evenings, at bedtime. He is therefore primarily a source of finance, when he has work. The mother has to look after the children's education, so academic achievement is often very poor.)

They all wanted something. Assailed on all sides, El Hadji made promises. To have some peace he gave them money for the cinema.

The maid came to tell him Modu was waiting.

Oumi N'Doye tried to catch her husband's eye. They were both absorbed in their separate obsessions. Oumi N'Doye's face showed her resentment. She folded her arms and watched her husband.

'Have a good day,' said El Hadji, looking up. His eyes met his wife's.

El Hadji was suddenly overcome with remorse and wanted to explain everything to her. As they went to the door he hoped she would say something; a joke or even a complaint. He would have responded and carried her off to the bedroom. In a tired, humble voice he would have told her:

'Oumi, I am impotent. Please, if you are the cause, release me. I'll buy you a car. I'll divorce N'Gone, if that is what you want. I beg you in the name of Yalla, release me!'

On the threshold he turned round and looked at her. Oumi said nothing, in insolent defiance. She stuck out her chin arrogantly and the whites of her eyes shone with an oily gleam.

Regretfully El Hadji decided he must go.

Modu observed his employer's troubles with compassion. He was afraid of offending him by being the first to refer to the *xala*. During the journey, his heart beating fast, he sang the praises of a marabout who lived near his home. He could vouch for him and for his ability.

*　　*　　*

Three days later.

The baobabs, with their squat trunks and their thick, leafless branches; the slender palms, straight and elegant, topped with their broad leaves; the parasol trees, spreading their dry-season foliage, a haven for animals, shepherds and farmers, and a resting-place for birds; the yellow, dry grass, broken at its roots; stumps of millet and maize stalks, indicating the boundaries of the ancient *lougans*; ghost-like trees, burnt by repeated bush fires. Beneath the torrid heat of the sun nature was covered with a thin layer of greyish dust, streaked by the rough tongue of the wind. The landscape was marked by a grandiose, calm austerity and harmony.

Modu was driving. He did not slow down at bends, or hardly at all. The Mercedes was travelling at top speed, the tyres shrieked at all the corners.

The scenery was changing all the time. The greyish terrain was scattered with ant-heaps of different shapes which, in the early morning and at dusk, worked on the imaginations and simple minds of the local people. Aggressive, stunted trees, bristling with thorns, marked the boundaries of the fields. The paths met, separated and ran parallel to each other towards the villages and the wells. The majestic silk-cotton trees, with their crazy roots running along the ground, formed a succession of enclosures.

The car turned off the tarred road and onto a dirt track. El Hadji wound up the windows. The winding track ran between a double hedge of *ngeer* trees. At the end of it they came to a small village. It was midday. People were asleep under a silk-cotton tree. Hearing the sound of the engine some looked up, wondering. The more daring approached it. The children admired and commented.

Modu spoke to an elderly peasant with a pock-marked face and wearing a simple caftan. The peasant flung his arms about in all directions as he spoke, as if he couldn't find his hands. Another peasant, a very tall man with a worn face, joined them. Modu returned to the car and spoke to El Hadji.

'Sereen Mada has gone to live in another village. To reach it we shall have to hire a cart.'

'What for?' asked El Hadji, who had remained in the car.

'The village is in the middle of the plain. A car couldn't get to it.'

'All right,' agreed El Hadji, climbing out of the Mercedes and looking around him. He exchanged greetings with the villagers. He was subjected to a minute inspection. 'It is someone important,' he heard them saying. He was invited to take a seat on the tree-trunk that served as a work-bench.

The man with the pock-marked face came back with a cart. The horse was extremely thin and had a brown coat covered with sores that had been smeared with blue. The driver invited the 'boss' to sit next to him. Modu sat behind, with his back to the direction in which they were going. After a while the driver began chatting to Modu. They found they had mutual acquaintances. The peasant hated the town because of all the machines. 'It is a rhythm of madness,' he said. Sereen Mada was the local celebrity. A man of knowledge. He only worked for 'bosses'. In fact one of them had tried to get him to go to the town with him, to keep him there for his personal use. 'Can you imagine such selfishness?'

El Hadji Abdou Kader Beye had shooting pains in his head. He was wet through with perspiration. The midday sun poured its heat onto him. He had to keep wiping his face with his fine linen handkerchief. The waves of heat rose in a misty vapour to the empty sky, torturing his eyes that were unaccustomed to it.

The horse went at a snail's pace, encouraged by the driver who at every step it took announced:

'We haven't much further to go.'

Then, as they emerged from a ravine, they saw conical thatched roofs, grey-black with weathering, standing out against the horizon in the middle of the empty plain. Free-ranging, skinny cattle with dangerous-looking horns fenced with one another to get at what little grass there was. No more than silhouettes in the distance, a few people were busy around the only well.

The driver of the cart was in familiar territory and greeted people as they passed. Sereen Mada's house, apart from its imposing size, was identical in construction with all the others. It was situated in the centre of the village whose huts were arranged in a semi-circle, which you entered by a single main entrance. The village had neither shop nor school nor dispensary; there was nothing at all attractive about it in fact. Its life was based on the principles of community interdependence.

They were received with the customary courtesy of this society, all the more so as his European dress meant that El Hadji was a stranger and a man of wealth. They were led into a hut which was unfurnished except for spotlessly clean mats laid on the ground. A second door opened onto another yard which was enclosed by a fence made of millet stalks. Beyond, a newly thatched, rectangular-shaped roof blocked the view. El Hadji was impatient to know what was happening. He felt disagreeably like an outsider.

A neatly dressed young woman with shining white teeth brought them water to quench their thirst. She kneeled in front of them before setting down the calabash and addressing them. The water was clear and on the surface floated small *seep* roots. When the young woman left them Modu held the calabash up to El Hadji.

'This is good, pure water.'

'I am not thirsty,' replied El Hadji, who was seated on one of the mats.

Deferentially Modu drank deeply and leaned back against the wall. He was soon asleep and snoring. This unseemly noise irritated El Hadji. He turned to look out into the distance but was unable to escape the sound. The last part of the journey had made him very tired. He unlaced his shoes and pulled them off. He undid his tie, glancing as he did so at his chauffeur. Leaning against the centre-pole, he reflected. He had little faith in all these charlatans. They were only after his money. He had lost count of how much he had spent. The only one in whom he had any faith at all was the *seet-katt*. When Modu had spoken to him about Sereen Mada he had been unconvinced. But his employee's arguments had sounded credible, and he had allowed himself to be led here, to this tiny room. Now all Modu could do was go off to sleep.

Soon he too fell asleep.

The muezzin had called the faithful to the *Takkusan* and *Timis* prayers, and the *Geewe* prayer was also over. The shadows grew darker. Objects became indistinct. One by one the stars began to take up their positions in the sky above. There was complete darkness when El Hadji woke with a start.

'Modu! Modu!' he called urgently. 'Have you any matches?'

He heard a rustling of clothes. Modu felt about his person and finally produced a tiny, pointed flame. It grew smaller, spread out at the base, then obstinately leapt into life again, climbing, moving, dancing to a point with a bluish crown.

El Hadji looked at his watch.

'We have slept a long time, boss.'

The room went dark again.

'We need a light,' grumbled El Hadji, who had found his shoes.

'*Assalamaleku*! You are awake?' asked a woman's voice coming from the first door.

She was holding a storm-lamp in one hand. All they could see was the fork of her legs escaping from under her cloth. The top of her body merged with the darkness. She placed the lamp next to the entrance, beside the calabash of water. She went on: 'We did not want to wake you. There is water in the enclosure for you to wash, if you wish. I have brought you something to eat. Please excuse our cooking.'

A little girl, who had been waiting behind her, placed a wooden bowl covered with a winnowing fan on the ground. They withdrew, leaving the lamp.

'We are not going to spend the night here,' said El Hadji.

'Boss, you must be patient. Sereen Mada knows we are here.'

El Hadji regretted having spoken as he had done and lied:

'I have things to do in Dakar.'

Swarms of fireflies were flitting around the glass of the lamp. Modu went out to the toilet.

Left alone El Hadji felt crushed by the silence. Modu returned and placed the wooden bowl between them. He lifted the fan: it was a mutton couscous. El Hadji declined to eat any of it.

'I'm not hungry. But if I'd foreseen this situation I'd have come prepared.'

'You haven't had anything to eat all day, boss. Drink some water at least. I assure you it is quite safe.'

El Hadji was very thirsty. The ice-hamper with his bottles of mineral water had been left behind in the Mercedes. Modu, a child of the earth, ate with appetite. The couscous had been very well prepared and the grains did not stick together.

The dim light crudely accentuated their features. The floor gave off a warm smell. Through the two facing doors the sky was full of stars. They could hear whispering outside. Someone came to take them to Sereen Mada. They crossed three enclosures before they reached him. He was waiting for them, seated on a mat on the ground. A paraffin lamp, standing a little way behind him, lit up his clothes from the back. Sereen Mada himself merged with the darkness.

'*Bismilax.*'

He invited them to sit down on a mat facing him.

Modu, familiar with the correct etiquette, had removed his shoes and with both hands devoutly shook and kissed Sereen Mada's hand. El Hadji ostentatiously imitated him. After a lengthy exchange of courtesies Sereen Mada apologised unctuously. An urgent affair had required his presence. As soon as he had returned he had gone to 'visit' them. They were asleep. Sleep is good for the body. A pity it makes us forget Yalla. He himself no longer slept.

He addressed Modu:

'Are the intentions healthy that have guided your step to this humble concession?'

'Healthy intentions only, master. Seated here before you is my employer. He is also more than a friend. He has been suffering from a *xala* for weeks, months. This *xala* alone brings us to you. We have come humbly as your followers to beg for your benevolent assistance.'

Modu gave details about the life of his 'more-than-a-friend', as if he were the client. El Hadji grunted confirmation of what his employee said.

'This kind of curse is very complicated. Very complicated. You must realize that knowledge of such things is like a well. Wells don't all have the same depth and their water does not have the same taste. This sort of curse is my speciality. But only Yalla can do anything about it. I shall try but you must pray with me. Let us beg for Yalla's gentle intercession.'

When he had finished speaking he called one of his disciples, who emerged from the dark, near the main hut. The master whispered something to him. The lad went out. Addressing the patient Sereen Mada told him what his fee would be and said that a heifer would be needed for the sacrifice. The fee was agreed. El Hadji had no cash on him. Sereen Mada knew what a cheque was. By the light of the lamp El Hadji wrote one out for him. El Hadji's fellow businessmen settled with him in the same manner. The disciple returned with a cloth, which Sereen Mada said he had obtained from the Holy One who lived a long, long way from there, near the foothills of the Atlas mountains. He instructed El Hadji to remove all his clothes, including his greegrees. After a moment's hesitation El Hadji undressed. 'Fortunately it is dark,' he thought. The marabout made him lie on his back and covered him up to the neck with the cloth. Crouching near the prostrate man's head he said his beads.

El Hadji listened to the clicking of the beads as they fell at regular intervals onto one another. He looked up at the curved roof. Suddenly he felt as if he were on edge. A long-forgotten sensation made him break into bursts of shivering. It was as if sap was rising violently inside his body, running through its fibres and filling it right to his burning head. It went on coming in waves. Then he had the impression that he was being emptied. Slowly he relaxed and a liquid flowed through his veins towards his legs. All his being now became concentrated in the region of his loins. It caused an effervescence which startled him. Shakily his penis rose by degrees until it was stiff. Lifting

his head and craning his neck, he looked down at it where it was covered by the cloth.

'Modu! Modu! Look!' he cried, overcome with astonishment.

'*Alhamdoullilah!*' exclaimed Modu with immense satisfaction, as if it was he himself who was being cured.

Sereen Mada passed the palm of his hand over El Hadji's scalp and face. His soft hand smelt strongly of musk.

'Move your ears,' ordered Sereen Mada.

El Hadji obeyed. He was overjoyed. He discovered he had ears. His whole body was tingling with life.

'It is over. The curse is broken,' said Sereen Mada.

El Hadji dressed. He was full of gratitude for the master.

'I have your cheque. What I have taken away I can restore equally quickly,' said Sereen Mada, returning to his original place.

El Hadji Abdou Kader Beye, talking volubly, promised heaven and earth. He swore that his bank account had sufficient funds to meet the cheque.

The night had grown older.

El Hadji was in a hurry to get back to Dakar. His virility was restored and he was thinking of his third wife. A messenger was sent to wake the cart-driver, who came with his ancient horse. On the return journey a euphoric El Hadji chatted with the driver. His blood was hot.

*　　*　　*

It was day when they reached Dakar. Seeing two policemen, Modu slowed down the car.

He shared the joyous, good-natured mood of his employer who, cheered by his cure, told him without inhibition of his weeks and months of misery. Happy and jovial, and with plenty of exaggeration, he described the ill-effects of the *xala*. He was regenerated, brimming with vigour. He could barely contain his desire. As they drove through the town he admired the buildings, the people in the streets, the bright colours.

'At which villa shall I drop you, boss? At which port of call?' teased Modu.

The 'at which villa' had taken him by surprise, interrupting the warm flow of his inner excitement. In effect, he had three villas and three wives, but where was his real *home*? At the houses of the three wives he was merely 'passing through.' Three nights each! He had nowhere a corner of his own into which he could withdraw and be alone. With each of his wives everything began and ended with the bed. Was he having second thoughts? Were these profound reflections? Whatever it was it left him with an after-taste of regret.

'At which villa?' he repeated to himself. At Adja Awa Astou's? There was nothing simple about that woman's simplicity. She was deeply religious and lived according to the teachings of her Muslim faith, accomplishing her conjugal duties with wifely obedience.

Oumi N'Doye's? A volcano! She would get every advantage she could from an unexpected visit, seeing it as a mark of preference, and would demand more such visits.

N'Gone's? In her case he had an insult to get off his chest. That Badyen woman had flouted him too much. The whole family was living on him like jiggers. How had that third marriage come about? A spark of lucidity flashed through his mind. 'N'Gone is certainly attractive. But what really had drawn him to her? Was it the demon of middle-age? Was he nothing but a pleasure-seeker?'

He could find no answer. But he was sure now that he had never had any real feeling for her. Narcissism? He took stock and congratulated himself on having faced the danger and overcome it. He made his decision: he would finish with all this virginity hocus-pocus. It was proving too expensive.

'To the third's place!'

'At last!' sighed Modu, putting his foot on the accelerator.

The Badyen was the first to see him get out of the Mercedes, his suit crumpled, his hair ruffled, his face dirty, his shoes – like the car – covered in dust. A rapid but thorough inspection told her that the man had recovered his virility.

'*Alhamdoullilah*!' she cried, putting on a face to suit the occasion. 'I knew you would "free" yourself! How did you do it? Which of your wives was it?'

'*Alhamdoullilah*!' he replied, reaching the verandah in a single energetic bound.

Yay Bineta, the Badyen, followed close at his heels.

'El Hadji, listen! N'Gone started her period last night,' she said, entering the bedroom with him. She kept the door ajar.

The room was lit by a bright light, down to the feet of the dressed tailor's dummy. The furnishings were exactly as they had been. N'Gone woke up.

'What did you say?' exclaimed the man, staring at the Badyen.

'I said N'Gone was not available at the moment. She started her period last night. N'Gone, you tell him.'

'It is true. It started yesterday. It's given me a stomach-ache,' N'Gone explained in French.

El Hadji refused to believe them. Rearing like a stallion he confronted the Badyen in a silent duel. The latent repulsion he felt for the woman and which he had always kept in check welled up violently. His aversion was evident in the hardness of his look. It was this woman who had instigated this third marriage, he told himself. It was she too who had prevented him from having N'Gone before they were married. If N'Gone had always managed to slip through his fingers, it was because she, the Badyen, was there in the shadows, advising and prompting her. El Hadji cursed himself for having been such a weak fool.

'Do you want to see her linen?' asked the Badyen, knowing very well that the man would not go so far as to insist on seeing this piece of cloth.

El Hadji looked with severity at each of the two women in turn. 'It is someone close to you.' With this thought in his mind he hurried out.

Yay Bineta ran after him.

'El Hadji, believe us! It is true! Listen, I must speak to you.'

In the car he ordered his chauffeur:

'To Oumi N'Doye's.'

He could no longer hear what the Badyen was saying.

At his second wife's villa his arrival did not seem to cause surprise. Oumi N'Doye dragged him off to 'her' room. They spent the whole day and night in bed, to the woman's great satisfaction.

*   *   *

The next morning, shaved, wearing a 'Prince of Wales' suit, and his black shoes well polished, El Hadji breakfasted with appetite: the

76

juice of two oranges, eggs and ham, white coffee, bread and butter. The maid placed the bottle of mineral water on the table and withdrew. Oumi N'Doye was overjoyed to see her husband's knife and fork at work. She was in a seventh heaven, thrilled with these pleasures brought to her outside her own *moomé*.

'Shall I tell you something, El Hadji?' she said, her head gently resting on one hand, her elbows on the table.

El Hadji Abdou Kader Beye looked at his wife with an air of self-assurance. He wiped his lips with dabs of his serviette and said:

'I am listening.'

'I had heard you had the *xala*.'

El Hadji did not reply immediately. With a confident gesture he poured himself a glass of mineral water, looking at his wife.

'Who did you hear it from, that I had this *xala*?'

'People.'

'What people?'

'In the neighbourhood.'

'What do you think, wife?'

'Oh!' she cried, her mouth round, her eyes lowered with just a hint of modesty. Then raising her head: 'People have evil tongues. Why don't you stay and rest here today? You work too hard. Your hair is going white.'

'I am going to the office,' he said, rising.

'You will come back this evening? Just for a minute?'

'Oumi, it is not your *aye*.'

And he left her.

The faithful Modu was at the wheel. The Mercedes had not been cleaned.

'I'm sorry, boss, about the car. . .'

'Take me to the office, then you can see to it.'

Comfortably ensconced in the right-hand corner behind the driver, El Hadji contemplated the future with optimism and assurance. He was preoccupied with the question of divorcing his third wife, N'Gone. He felt vindictive and was determined to satisfy his urge for revenge. Calculating the expense occasioned by the wedding he decided his only course of action was to get her pregnant and then

77

repudiate her. The suspicion that the *xala* had been caused by the Badyen had become a certainty. That family had damaged his male honour. The whole town knew about his affliction. Happily he had regained his form.

The car-washer, standing on the edge of the pavement with a pail of water at his feet, watched Modu manœuvre to park the car. Rama had parked her Fiat in front. She too watched the chauffeur's manœuvring.

Father and daughter entered the shop.

'By my father's belt Modu, you must pay me 500 francs today,' said the car-washer after inspecting the car.

'Two hundred francs. Not a centime more.'

'You're the chauffeur of a big man, Modu. You shouldn't be stingy.'

'Leave it then. Someone else will wash the car!' Modu flung at him as he walked towards the shop.

He came back carrying his stool.

'Modu! Fear Yalla! I wash the car everyday for 100 francs. For today you must pay me at least a thousand francs. Look at that dirt! If you went to a *toubab* he'd charge you more than two thousand francs.'

The young man wiped his index finger across the wing. A long line appeared underneath it. He showed it to Modu.

'All right! I'll give you 300 francs,' the chauffeur agreed, settling himself not far from the beggar.

'Is it you, Modu?'

'Yes'.

'You have been away two days.'

'I was out of town with the boss.'

'Nothing serious I hope?'

'No.'

'*Alhamdoullilah!*' said the beggar.

He had not turned round. Modu could only see his hunched back, his prominent ears, his skinny neck. The beggar went on to ask:

'Is El Hadji in his office?'

'Yes.'

'I will lower my voice then.'

He intoned his holy complaint once more, in a carefully modulated

voice. It was the never-changing chant sung with softer inflexions of the voice.

Modu stretched out his legs and lit a cigarette. Leaning his head against the wall of the shop, he sat day-dreaming.

In the 'office' Rama struggled to keep her self-control. She was in a state of agitation. She knew she was powerless to stop her father's flow of words, which were so full of obvious lies she could not stand it. She kept her eyes lowered as her father spoke. El Hadji could only see her narrow, prominent forehead, which reminded him of his first wife, and the shining strips of scalp between the short plaits. Her father spoke hesitantly, the sentences did not come easily.

'I know it's your mother who sent you,' he repeated, as if to insinuate collusion between mother and daughter.

'I repeat, it is not so. Mother knows nothing about it. I came of my own accord. I know she is upset. At the moment she is eaten up with remorse about something. You must realize that I am old enough to know about certain things.'

'Know about what things?' asked her father, thinking of his *xala*.

Rama refused to reply, thinking it would be her mother who would suffer as a result. She was on the verge of bringing up everything she reproached him with, the third marriage, the *xala*. Looking away, she watched the progress of a cockroach towards the files.

'I know that mother is desperately unhappy,' she said, fully conscious of the hypocrisy and falseness of what she was saying, of lying to herself.

'Your mother is ill?'

'Physically, no.'

'I'll call round. Tell her that.'

Their eyes met.

'I won't tell her. Mother doesn't know that I have been to see you. I'm going.'

'Do you need anything?'

She had reached the door. She turned to look at him. The cockroach slipped in among the boxes and disappeared.

'Thank you, father, but it's mother who needs you.'

A few days previously Rama had gone to see her grandfather at

Gorée, accompanied by Pathé. Usually she went once a fortnight on Sunday, sometimes staying the night. The young girl's presence brought a breath of fresh air to the old colonial-style house with its wooden balcony.

Papa John had met them as usual in the garden, far from the tourists who invaded the island. It was cooler outside.

'*Maam* (grandfather), your daughter sends her greetings,' said Rama, as she always did.

'You always say the same thing. Renée. . .'

'Why can't you accept your daughter's new faith, *maam*? It's twenty years now. She isn't called Renée any more. She has also been to Mecca. She's Adja Awa Astou now.'

'That is why your father has taken a second and a third wife. Are you in favour of polygamy?'

'I am against it and he knows I am.'

'Yet you are a Muslim.'

'Yes, a modern Muslim. But *maam*, that isn't the problem. It's to do with your daughter. You don't even know your three youngest grandsons.'

'When Africa was Africa it was for the young to visit the old. I haven't set foot on the mainland for two years.'

'So even on All Saint's Day you don't visit grandmother's grave any more? There is no cemetery on Gorée.'

'I'll make my last crossing feet first then. Renée can come and keep me company.'

'Alas, no. Muslim women don't accompany the dead.'

'We'll meet before God, then,' said the old man. Turning to Pathé: 'I haven't offered you anything, doctor.'

'You shouldn't talk to him like that,' Pathé said to Rama when the old man had disappeared into the house.

Rama stuck her tongue out at him and called:

'*Maam*, I'll give you a hand.'

Left alone Pathé lit a cigarette. Rama returned with a tray, Papa John with the ice-bucket. The grandfather and his granddaughter had *pastis*, Pathé a beer.

'Your good health,' said the old man, spilling a few drops onto the ground as he raised the glass to his lips.

The conversation was relaxed. Papa John spoke about his life on the island. He talked about old times and the Feast of St Charles. He had hoped Rama would come to take him to the church. That year the feast had passed unmarked. There had been nothing to distinguish that Sunday from all the other Sundays. Holiday-makers, including many Europeans, had come to sunbathe on the warm sand of the beach. Papa John couldn't understand it at all: these Europeans who abandoned God's house for idleness. Hadn't they brought Catholicism to this country?

Nostalgically the grandfather evoked the pomp of the Feast of St Charles in the old days. There would be crowds of people, men and women, young and old, come from the four corners of the country, filling the tiny church. They came for a religious festival but the flags showed it was the island's feast-day as well. A band would march through the crowded streets, cheering the whole of Béer (the Wolof name for Gorée). After mass the women in long dresses, elbow-length gloves and English-style hats, and the men in frock coats or tails, top-hats and carrying gold-knobbed sticks, would make their way in a garden-party atmosphere to the town-hall for apéritifs. Those were the good old days. These recollections of the past made Papa John sad, his old eyes filled with tears. Island families were selling their houses to foreigners. The Europeans, the technical advisers, the directors and managers of companies who lived on the island now, did not go to church.

When her grandfather walked with them to the ferry, Rama tried to persuade him to visit her mother. She was convinced it was only absurd pride that made them maintain their positions.

'And how is your father?' asked Papa John.

Rama hesitated, uncertain how to reply. Was the question a trap? The vengeance of an embittered old man? Had her grandfather got wind of El Hadji's *xala*? Erect, looking straight ahead of him, Papa John waited for the reply to his question.

'I haven't seen my father since his third marriage.'

'Aren't you living at home any more?'

'Yes, I am. But I never see my father.'

'Then you know nothing of his *xala*?'

'I know that mother is very unhappy. If you came to see her now she would be very happy.'

'Why doesn't Renée come and live here?'

Papa John fell silent. He had stopped. The young couple did likewise.

'The house is hers. She can return to it whenever she likes. My last crossing will be feet first,' he repeated, setting off again.

They reached the jetty without exchanging another word.

The young couple embarked. The old man returned to his house alone, wrapped in his pride.

Depressed, Rama had nothing to say. Pathé understood how she felt. He too said nothing.

* * *

After his daughter's departure El Hadji realized she was now a young woman old enough to marry. Why didn't the doctor ask for her hand? El Hadji could visualize himself playing the generous father-in-law. He would give his consent without conditions of any kind and he would oppose excessive expense. For the celebration they would only invite a few close friends. 'Is Rama still a virgin?' he wondered. He quickly put the question out of his mind. He hadn't intended it. Today, for the first time in three months since he had slapped her on the afternoon of his wedding, they had had a serious conversation. Rama had been the only one who had dared oppose the marriage. Pity she was a girl. He would have been able to make something of her had she been a boy. Being a fatalist he thought of his two meetings with his daughter as strange coincidences: the last occasion was the day before his *xala* and today's was the day of his cure.

He would go to Adja Awa Astou. It was a long time since they had talked. She was such a taciturn woman, so indifferent to the things of this life that you could bury her alive and she would not complain.

His meditation over, he sent for Madame Diouf, to take stock of his business; it was time he turned his attention to more concrete matters. Madame Diouf told him where the gaps were and what they needed. The re-stocking of the shop had become a matter of urgency: there was nothing left. There were also the wages of his employees to be paid. She, Madame Diouf, had not been paid for more than two months. Why had she not reminded him? He sent for his chauffeur. The same story. They turned to the domestic side: petrol bills to pay, grocery bills (each wife had her own grocer), servants' wages, water and electricity. It was thanks to the intervention of a cousin of Madame Diouf that the latter had not been cut off. The water and electricity bills would have to be settled straight away. As for the shop, it was empty. The retailers were going elsewhere. The manufacturers and other suppliers were all refusing to deliver goods. The picture was bleak. Finally, she had to inform him of an urgent meeting that evening, at the Chamber, with his fellow businessmen. If the rumour was true, it was he who was in the hot seat. Why? Why? She knew nothing more. El Hadji's face took on a look of anger. He decided to go and see the President on the spot. Since the Mercedes was being washed, Modu hailed a taxi for him. He climbed in.

In the spacious waiting-room of the 'Businessmen's Group' offices, two old women and three men were already waiting. The President's secretary liked him because he was always so courteous, and he was able to convince her of his need to see the President urgently on a matter of great importance.

As soon as the door opened El Hadji stepped through, paying no attention to the grumblings of the others. The air-conditioning came to meet him. It was a very large room, with curios hanging on the walls and polished mahogany furniture.

'You should have phoned me,' remarked the President. He had a black baby face. 'Today I receive the general public.'

'So much the better,' said El Hadji firmly. 'Tell me what is going on. Why am I the subject of a meeting?'

'First, have you been able to do anything about your *xala*?'

'It's finished. Over and done with.'

'I am very pleased for your sake. As for this meeting, it is nothing to worry about. Your colleagues want to stop the rather serious prejudice you are causing them.'

'What prejudice?'

'Keep calm. In business you must have the Englishman's self-control, the American's flair, and the Frenchman's politeness. Here it is just you and me. You know me well. But between you and the others, I am only an arbitrator. The thing is your colleagues are having difficulties for which they hold you responsible. Firstly, dishonoured cheques, and secondly. . .'

'What?'

'Let me finish. I am only putting you in the picture. Then you'll be able to defend yourself this afternoon if necessary. I have been personally approached by the National Grain Board who, two weeks before your marriage, gave you a quota certificate for thirty tons of rice. This you re-sold, according to a practice which is perfectly acceptable. But where is the money? You did not pay the Grain Board on the due date. The Board, having been informed of your excessive spending, made further inquiries about you and suspended the Group's credit. The consequences of this very soon became apparent. We have lost the advantages we had, thanks to you. None of your colleagues can have his quota now without paying cash. The National Grain Board expects to be paid for the thirty tons of rice or it will hand the matter over to the police or take you to court.

The President had provided this explanation in a calm voice, like a pedantic professor giving an Algebra lesson to a class of mutes.

El Hadji had listened in silence. At first he looked only at the President's hand energetically stressing certain points. As the President spoke El Hadji's face clouded over. His look of discomfiture betrayed his misery.

'President, you know my position! My *xala*! Fortunately I am cured now. I implore you, postpone the meeting for a week, just long enough for me to sort things out,' said El Hadji with cunning servility.

'We'll expect you this evening. It is desirable you should be there,' said the President with an air of finality.

Outside the President's office, El Hadji reflected. What he had just heard was the result of discussions among his colleagues. He knew very well that he was being threatened by them. He himself had behaved in the same way towards one of their number whom they had wanted to expel on a previous occasion. Now it was his turn. The mood of satisfaction he had felt in the morning melted like *karité* butter in the sun. He was too shaken to notice the people around him. He returned to his 'office' on foot. A visit to 'his' bank was clearly necessary. A loan to fill the gap. The cost of thirty tons of rice. The deputy manager looked after the affairs of the businessmen. He phoned him. He obtained an appointment without any difficulty for the early afternoon. The promptness with which he had obtained the appointment augured well for a satisfactory outcome. He had a 'surface' again!

*   *   *

Madame Diouf had written out the cheques for the wages, the water, the electricity, the petrol, and the rents. El Hadji graced them with his elaborate signature, the fruit of days and nights of practice.

At midday, to rest after the active twenty-four hours spent with his second wife and in order to be fresh for his appointment at the bank, El Hadji went to Adja Awa Astou's. The first wife was not expecting him. She showed no enthusiasm at his appearance, any more than she seemed put out by it. El Hadji could not avoid a certain feeling of sympathy for her undemonstrative reception.. Adja Awa Astou had lost weight and the whites of her eyes seemed to spill over onto her thin face. The conversation did not stray beyond the superficial. The father asked twice for Rama. She no longer came home at midday but was back early in the evening. He thought his daughter had too much freedom and scolded her mother for permitting it.

After his customary siesta, he fetched his briefcase and was driven to the bank by Modu.

The deputy manager was a man of indeterminate age, with a smooth black face, eyes protected by gold-rimmed spectacles, and carefully combed hair. He wore a white shirt and a dark tie. He received El Hadji affably, installing him in an armchair next to a coffee-table on which lay a packet of cigarettes and a gold-plated lighter. He had studied at a French business school and had then done his probation in various African branches of the bank, the head-office of which was in Paris. Its aim was to assist the emergence of an African commercial middle-class. Anxious to play fair with El Hadji, the young man put him at ease by addressing him as 'elder brother', a Wolof sign of respect.

El Hadji Abdou Kader Beye addressed him with exaggerated familiarity in a persuasive tone of voice. He asked effusively after his family, calling him 'cousin', as if there were obvious family ties between them. The deputy manager did his best to express himself in Wolof. Through lack of practice his speech was so full of borrowed words that in the end he had to resort to French.

'Elder brother, I know I am not one of your close friends. You didn't invite me to your third marriage. All Dakar is talking about it!'

'Cousin, you must know how bad our African secretaries are. Your name is definitely on my address list.'

The deputy manager placed a cigarette in his holder and lit it.

The conversation dragged on. Delaying tactics . . . They broached various subjects, putting off and avoiding the real issue.

'Elder brother, I am listening,' said the banker.

He pushed his spectacles back with a finger. Was he hoping to catch him off his guard? The effect was immediate. El Hadji said nothing.

'Good. Well,' he said, hesitating for a moment, trying to find the best way of approaching the subject.

Then he began: 'Cousin, I need some working capital. Just five hundred thousand francs. I have plans for expansion and I want to make a survey of the market in the African quarter.

'Why do you need capital?'

'Why?' echoed El Hadji. 'To work. Look at this list of retail traders in the town.'

'I have a thick file on you. You have already had two overdrafts of half a million francs, exceeding the upper limit allowed for overdrafts. What did you do with the thirty tons of rice you had from the National Grain Board? You sold it. What happened to the money? You are living beyond your income: three villas, cars on hire-purchase. Since your third marriage your cheques haven't stopped bouncing.'

El Hadji Abdou Kader Beye could find nothing to say in his own defence. Shamefaced, he drew several times on his cigarette with an air of submission.

'Well, big brother,' said the young man breaking the silence with a superior smile.

In conciliatory manner, he continued: 'What are you planning to do, elder brother? You know, a bank is not a charitable organization.'

'True, bankers are not patrons,' replied El Hadji, more out of defiance than anything else. (He knew how to use his voice when it suited him.) 'A loud voice pays in this country,' he said to himself. And aloud: 'Well, cousin, what do you intend to do with me?'

'We support the development of African commerce. Ours is the only bank in the country working with businessmen like yourself. It is the only one that gives you its confidence. But you must agree, there are limits.'

'Cousin, you are saying nothing I don't know already. It is true you are the only bank that helps us. But without going too much into details, we businessmen only gather the crumbs. The sons of the country are kept from the business that really makes money.'

88

'Perhaps, elder brother. Is that a reason for wasting the money you borrow? A bank has its rules. We can only lend to people who can offer security.'

'By which you mean I have none left?'

'Elder brother, that was not what I meant.'

'I am being frank with you. I know you are not altruists. But cousin, you must do something to help me.'

'Elder brother, I can promise nothing. I have to consult my superiors, you must understand. How much do you say you need?'

'Half a million.'

The deputy manager took the file from him, saying: 'Phone me late tomorrow morning, elder brother.'

'Cousin, I shall be hoping. Until tomorrow.'

'Until tomorrow.'

El Hadji decided he still had some punches left to pull. He was not defeated yet. This visit to the bank was like a prolongation of his life. He wasn't worried about the bounced cheques. 'They never prosecute anyone for letting cheques bounce,' he said to himself. But just to make sure he phoned a friend who was a magistrate. He had not been drawn to the attention of the court. He checked at the court for commercial cases as well. Nothing. He phoned a bailiff. Nothing there either concerning him.

El Hadji Abdou Kader Beye was relieved.

* * *

The lights in the square and the two lamps flanking the monumental staircase were reflected in the cars parked outside the Chamber. The drivers were talking in groups. Seeing the cars, El Hadji knew he was expected. The Mercedes had barely drawn up before he was out and climbing the steps to the entrance. His arrival in the conference chamber halted the conversation. He shook hands with the men standing round the large green table. They all knew one another. They were the same men who had attended his wedding. The chandelier threw its light onto the dozen or so heads.

'I think we are all here now. At any rate we have a quorum,' said the President, opening the meeting.

A few moments were spent deciding who should act as secretary for

90

the meeting, signing the attendance sheet, announcing the names of the proxy voters. Finally the real discussion began. Everyone spoke about El Hadji. Underhand dealings. Embezzlement. Moral harm. They demanded an example, to restore their discredited honour. Only recently one of their number had taken on the onerous office of President of the Chamber of Commerce and the die-hard neo-colonialists were intent on regaining control of it.

Kebe, a man with skin the colour of a ripe banana, a long face and a thin voice, spoke:

'For our honour's sake, El Hadji Abdou Kader Beye must be expelled from our Group. There are too many obstacles in our way. The banks insult us to our faces, they blame us for living according to feudal customs, they accuse us of negligence, of incompetence. Why? And now El Hadji, through his indiscretion, discredits us and our Group. There is in my view a good case for expelling him.'

Kebe sat down. The scraping of a match could be heard in the silence that followed.

'I agree,' said Diagne, whose jaws bulged at the sides of his face. His guttural, growling voice filled the room. He pushed out his chest and went on: 'We know El Hadji has sold the thirty tons of rice. What has he done with the money? He has taken a third wife! Because of him, and him alone, none of us has been able to obtain credit for weeks. Overdrafts? Capital? Nothing! We know how important honesty is in our profession. His lack of conscience about his cheques is a matter for the banks and his creditors. There is only one course of action: we must dissociate ourselves from him.'

'You are talking too fast, Diagne,' complained the secretary of the meeting.

Diagne was a little out of breath, the folds of his fat neck were rippling.

El Hadji felt as if he were in court facing a row of judges. His colleagues were treating him as if he were a total stranger.

'What was I saying?' asked Diagne, who was opposite El Hadji.

'We must dissociate ourselves from him.'

'Thank you, Mr Secretary. Dissociate ourselves from him, that's what we must do! We must write to the bank and tell them that El Hadji is no longer a member of our Group. As for the National Grain

Board, we will insist that they take the matter to court. Our Group has a duty to clear itself of this stain.'

Someone else spoke. He followed the same blustering line of reasoning. Like all of them he was concerned about the welfare of 'the people'. El Hadji felt as if he were an abcess which had to be lanced. He had the right to speak.

'We are listening.'

He was confused. For a few seconds he found it difficult to say anything, uncertain what approach to adopt. He began almost in a murmur, his ideas all in a muddle.

'Who is accusing me? What am I accused of?'

Unexpected! No one replied. This moment of surprise restored his confidence. Sure of himself, he looked around questioningly.

'What are we? Mere agents, less than petty traders! We merely re-distribute. Re-distribute the remains the big men deign to leave us. Are we businessmen? I say no! Just clodhoppers!'

'I protest, Mr President,' intervened Laye. 'He is insulting us. You eat from the same dungheap as we do. Go and preach to others.'

There was a general uproar; everyone wanted to speak. El Hadji controlled himself. A pleasant warmth spread through his body. It was an inner joy that woke in him memories of his militant days. No doubt his old aggressiveness had been blunted by his cars, his villas, his bank account and the mineral water, but he knew he had touched his colleagues on a sore spot.

'Order! Gentlemen, order!' shouted the President, banging the table with his gavel. 'Order! Come along now! There is no need to take offence, gentlemen.'

'El Hadji thinks he is still living in colonial times. Those days when he harangued the crowds with his trickery are over, well and truly over. We are independent now. We are the ones who govern. You collabor-ate with the régime that's in power. So stop all this empty, stupid talk about foreign control.'

'Mr President, may I finish?' El Hadji asked, fully in control of himself.

'Yes, El Hadji.'

'Isn't that true, Laye?'

'No asides! Put your case!' roared Laye.

'All right. We are a bunch of clodhoppers. Who owns the banks?

92

The insurance companies? The factories? The businesses? The wholesale trade? The cinemas? The bookshops? The hotels? All these and more besides are out of our control. We are nothing better than crabs in a basket. We want the ex-occupier's place? We have it. This Chamber is the proof. Yet what change is there really in general or in particular? The colonialist is stronger, more powerful than ever before, hidden inside us, here in this very place. He promises us the left-overs of the feast if we behave ourselves. Beware anyone who tries to upset his digestion, who wants a bigger profit. What are we? Clodhoppers! Agents! Petty traders! In our fatuity we call ourselves "businessmen"! Businessmen without funds.'

'You have gone on long enough, El Hadji,' interrupted Diop, a bald man with a shiny, bumpy head. 'We aren't at the theatre. You're up to your neck in muck and you preach revolution to us. You should have thought of all that before. Let's get it over. Let's vote his expulsion.'

The hum spread, grew louder. They were all talking at once.

After Diop's interruption El Hadji had lost the thread of his argument. His thoughts became confused again. He looked at the faces around him for agreement and support. He saw Sheikh Ba scribbling something. Sheikh Ba was not a man who wasted his time. It was whispered that he had the ear of the great of the land. He finished writing. El Hadji was intrigued by the journey of the piece of paper as it passed from hand to hand. It reached the President, who unfolded it. El Hadji shivered with anxiety. He looked hard at the President. Impossible to read the contents of the note in his face. El Hadji was sure that if he had Sheikh Ba's support he would be all right.

'El Hadji, have you finished speaking?' asked the President.

'No.'

'We are listening.'

'I'll be brief,' he said, speaking in a dull, flat voice, without resonance, which bore no resemblance to his normal voice. He glanced towards Sheikh Ba before continuing.

'All of us here have signed cheques that have bounced, sold quotas.'

'We have been insulted enough! Mr President, tell us whose side you are on.'

The President wondered if Laye's question was a disguised threat.

93

Perhaps he had let El Hadji talk too long, allowed him to say things that should only be said in private.

'Well, before we reach a decision, I have a proposal from our friend Sheikh Ba,' said the President, giving in.

'I beg your pardon, Mr President, for interrupting you. It is indeed a proposal. I was drawing your attention to certain points of fact.'

When Sheikh Ba raised points of fact at meetings, everyone knew he was intending to guide the discussion along a particular line with a definite end in view.

'We can request the withdrawal of El Hadji's import-export licence on the grounds we already know, but also our... well, he has not paid his dues to the Group for some time. His expulsion depends entirely on us. The trickiest problem will doubtless be our future relations with the National Grain Board. If we show ourselves to be decisive and firm in the decision we are about to take, I believe the National Grain Board would have no further grounds for complaint against us. So we would return to where we were before. As far as the matter of dishonoured cheques is concerned, that does not depend on us. I understand – it's what is being said – El Hadji has a very thick file in a certain place. Mr President, these are the points of fact I had in mind.'

Sheikh Ba's intervention terminated the discussion. El Hadji had nothing to say. They voted unanimously for his exclusion from their Group.

He was left standing on his own.

With dignity, he descended the stairs.

'To Adja's,' he ordered Modu.

In the car he felt ill at ease. His sudden downfall caught him in the stomach. Without remembering very clearly what he had discussed with Rama, one sentence came back into his mind: 'Our country is a plutocracy.'

At the 'Villa Adja Awa Astou,' mother and daughter were in the sitting-room.

'Good evening,' he said.

'Good evening,' they replied.

El Hadji went over to his daughter and looked over her shoulder.

'What's that?'

'Wolof.'

'You write in Wolof?'

94

'Yes. We have a newspaper called *Kaddu* and we teach anyone who wants to learn how to write in Wolof.'

'Do you think it will be adopted as the language of the country?'

'Eighty-five per cent of the people speak it. They only need to know how to write it.'

'What about French?'

'An historical accident. Wolof is our national language.'

El Hadji smiled and went over to his wife.

'How are you?'

'Well, thanks be to Yalla!'

'Get me something to drink, please.'

Adja Awa Astou got up and disappeared into the kitchen.

'I came,' said El Hadji, addressing his daughter.

'I see, father.'

Adja Awa Astou returned with a bottle of mineral water and a glass. She served her husband, then told him:

'Yay Bineta came to see you.'

'What did she want?'

'She wanted to see you.'

'I will go tomorrow.'

'She told me that "they" would wait all night for you if necessary.'

Rama gathered up her books.

'Pass the night in peace.'

'You too pass the night in peace,' replied her mother.

'I shall go and see them tomorrow,' reiterated the father, loud enough for Rama to hear.

Adja Awa Astou said nothing. She went to bed first, leaving her husband alone.

*   *   *

El Hadji Abdou Kader Beye woke up a little earlier than usual. He watched the children leave for school. Alassane helped them into the mini-bus.

The road-sweeper's cart passed by.

'Papa,' called Mariem, Oumi N'Doye's younger daughter.

The father went out to them. Each of the second wife's children held out a hand to him.

95

'How is your mother?'

'She is well,' replied Mariem.

'Papa, are you thinking about mother's car?' asked the youngest child.

Rama nervously put her foot down twice on the accelerator.

'I'm thinking about it. I promised your mother.'

'When will it be?'

'When? Soon,' replied El Hadji without conviction, drawing away.

'Father always lets us down,' remarked Mariem to her brother as the vehicle moved off.

Modu dropped El Hadji at his 'office'. They arrived at the same time as Madame Diouf. As soon as he had seated himself at his table El Hadji phoned the bank. He could not wait until the end of the morning, he was too impatient. He was informed that the deputy manager was very busy and told to phone the following week to make an appointment. The woman's voice very politely suggested he stay calm. He insisted, but in vain. After they had argued for fifteen minutes he realized that there was no intention of receiving him.

Madame Diouf came in to announce a visitor.

'Who is it?'

'A *toubab* representing "Automobile Credit".'

He told her to show him in. The European was dressed in a cotton shirt and khaki trousers and carried a fat briefcase made of snakeskin.

'You recognize me?' he asked as soon as he was seated opposite El Hadji.

'Of course.'

'I apologize for calling so early. I don't want to take up too much of your time, so I'll come to the point. . .'

Opening his briefcase he took out a cardboard file, which he placed on his lap. He waved away the flies with his hand.

'Mr El Hadji Abdou Kader Beye, you have made no payments on your cars for three months now. I have been sent to find out why.'

'True,' said El Hadji, anxious to gain the advantage with a prompt reply. 'True. You are quite right. I have been very busy these last months. Please excuse my lateness. I received your reminders. I understand there is a five per cent interest charge when this happens.'

El Hadji took out his personal cheque-book.

'Please, Mr El Hadji Abdou Kader Beye,' said the whiteman with a

96

slight gesture of his hand and speaking in a tone of voice which had a hidden authority, enough to stop El Hadji's intention. 'Please, sir,' he repeated, with a hint of a smile at the corners of his mouth. 'I don't want to hide from you, sir, the fact that we have been told about your financial situation.'

They remained frozen, each with his thoughts. El Hadji read in the whiteman's face a determination to bend him, to bring him to his knees. When the representative's mocking look disappeared El Hadji felt the shock even more strongly. He scrutinized the fellow again but could not really make out what was going on in his mind.

The beggar's wail could be heard.

'Can you tell me who informed you?' asked El Hadji.

'You must know that over the phone you don't see the face.'

'The voice? The accent?'

El Hadji was certain they were trying to catch him out. He smiled, a sceptical smile that distorted his mouth.

The whiteman looked at him for a moment and evaded the question.

'I merely wanted to warn you. The sooner you settle with us the better.'

'What do you mean by "the sooner you settle"?'

'Three days.'

'Can you give me a little more time than that?'

'I understand. Unfortunately I am only a messenger. I have my instructions.'

When the representative from "Automobile Credit" left him, El Hadji sat in silent anger. Mentally he counted his influential contacts: someone in a high position or having a lot of influence, who could intercede on his behalf. He was like a mouse caught in a trap trying to find a way to escape. His *xala*, his third wife were pushed to the back of his mind. In a broken sequence he recalled his efforts to better himself. He had schemed and struggled to get where he was, to be somebody. And now it was all collapsing around him.

Madame Diouf gave a hesitant knock and timidly entered the 'office'.

'Sir,' she said.

El Hadji looked up wearily at her.

'Yes?'

She was embarrassed.

'Sir, the bank returned the cheque to me,' she said, looking at the floor as she placed the cheque on the table.

'Oh!' he said blankly.

'You know I need the money. For two months I have been living on credit at home. I must pay my rent. If I don't pay it this week my family and I will. . . will. . .'

She stopped, unable to continue.

'Give me two days, Madame Diouf. I am going through a bad patch at the moment. Will you?'

She nodded agreement.

'Come in!' called El Hadji.

It was Modu, accompanied by a man wearing a worn-out caftan and a cap made of black wool with a tassel hanging down one side. He had rings of plaited leather around his neck and red, mobile eyes.

'I have been sent by Sereen Mada,' he declared with self-assurance, standing well clear of the table. His attitude verged on contempt.

Madame Diouf withdrew.

'Sereen Mada?' repeated El Hadji examining the intruder, who was unknown to him. He asked: 'Who is Sereen Mada?'

The fellow in the woollen cap gave a shiver of surprise, opened wide his eyes and looked hard at Modu. Modu lowered his head like a faithful dog in front of its master.

'The person who treated you and cured your *xala*.'

'Oh, yes.'

The 'oh, yes' came like a gasp from El Hadji, who quickly straightened himself and invited the man to sit down.

'I hope he is well. As it happens I need to see him urgently. How is he?'

'*Alhamdoullilah!*'

Joy and hope surged up inside El Hadji. He had confidence in Sereen Mada. Only he could get him out of his present predicament. Why had he not thought of him sooner?

'Sit down, my friend. Brother. Please excuse my ill manners. You must know how terrible life is in N'Dakaru! You have come at just the right moment. I need Sereen Mada's help very urgently. We will go to his village together. While you are in N'Dakaru, please by my guest. Modu will drive you to my second wife's villa. No. . . take him to Adja Awa Astou, Modu. She's my first. She is very religious. A woman!

Sit down, and tell me what Sereen Mada wants,' asked El Hadji finally.

'To give you this,' said the fellow, holding out the cheque to him. 'I have just been to the bank. Remember what Sereen Mada told you. What he has taken away, he can restore.'

El Hadji Abdou Kader Beye walked up and down his 'office', entangling himself in vague explanations.

The other, indifferent to all his excuses, with a reproving look placed the cheque beside Madame Diouf's and left.

'Boss, didn't you recognize Sereen Mada? It was him!' Modu told him after he had gone.

'Who? Sereen Mada?'

'Yes. Before he came in he told me not to say who he was.'

El Hadji Abdou Kader Beye rushed outside. Sereen Mada was nowhere in sight. El Hadji was petrified. He was oblivious to the noise of the lorries, the handcarts, the cries. He returned wearily to his 'office'.

In the taxi Sereen Mada took his beads from his pocket. It was a long rosary with ebony beads encrusted with silver thread. He prayed furiously. His eyes were closed but his lips were busy. He was restoring El Hadji's *xala*.

*   *   *

Modu returned to his place on the stool with a faraway look in his eyes.

'What is happening, Modu?' asked the beggar.

'Sereen Mada has just left.'

'A courtesy visit?'

'If you like,' replied the chauffeur, his head against the wall, his legs outstretched.

'Be more explicit, Modu.'

Modu drew himself up. Crossing his legs, he leaned over to the beggar and put his mouth to his ear:

'Perhaps you don't know, or do you? El Hadji has had the *xala* since his third marriage. Sereen Mada cured him. Now El Hadji can't pay him. I am sure Sereen Mada is going to give him back his *xala* later this evening.'

'I have heard of Sereen Mada. They say he is a man of his word. The *xala* is nothing. I can remove it.'

Modu smiled sceptically. He scrutinized the beggar from behind. Sensing he was being watched, the latter did not move.

'You don't believe me do you, Modu?'

'It's not that,' replied the chauffeur. 'El Hadji hasn't any money to pay you.'

'I don't want to be paid.'

'You would take away his *xala* for nothing? Free? Just like that?'

'I didn't say that. I wouldn't ask him for money. But he would have to do my bidding.'

'You worry me.'

'If El Hadji does what I tell him he will be cured. He will become a man like you and me.'

More intrigued than ever, Modu gazed at the back of the beggar's neck. The beggar intoned his chant keeping a proud, distant pose.

* * *

El Hadji Abdou Kader Beye got his *xala* back. Not knowing which way to turn in the face of so much adversity, he sought refuge at his first wife's villa. It was in a family setting, with his *awa*, that he felt secure. As usual Adja Awa Astou asked for no explanation. She welcomed him as if she had expected him to return soon. She told the children their father was unwell and needed some peace and quiet. Obediently they went about the house on tip-toe.

For days on end El Hadji sat on the settee, his arms stretched out on either side of him, his mind far away.

His creditors besieged him. The National Grain Board began legal proceedings. 'Automobile Credit' re-possessed the wedding-present car, the mini-bus and the Mercedes. The estate agent sent bailiffs to expropriate the villas. They were days of misery for this man accustomed to living in style.

Every morning and afternoon he saw the children set off for school on foot. Rama, whose Fiat had not been re-possessed as it was in her name, was kept very busy ferrying her younger brothers about.

Madame Diouf had laid a complaint before the Labour Tribunal. El Hadji failed to attend the two hearings. He was found guilty in his absence for contempt of court and the matter handed over to the bailiffs. The latter were intransigent, refusing to allow him any time. Adja Awa Astou sold her jewelry to help out. He was besieged on all sides, completely isolated. Only Modu remained loyal. The chauffeur, who was a man of feeling, was reluctant to leave him, to abandon the slowly sinking ship.

Yay Bineta, the Badyen, came for 'news' as she put it. After the exchange of traditional Wolof courtesies, Adja Awa Astou had left them, saying she had work to do. As soon as she was alone with him the Badyen attacked El Hadji in language full of innuendo. With great eloquence she told him how angry she and N'Gone had been. There she was, night after night, by herself in a cold bed. Was he not her husband? What then were his real intentions?

The Badyen watched him, unobserved, as she spoke. Her widow's instinct – the instinct of a woman left on her own – detected the smell of wrinkled skin emanating from the male sitting at the table beside her. Folds of malice appeared at the base of her nose, between her eyes.

'Is it true the water and electricity are going to be cut off because the bills have not been paid? A man from the court came to see the villa.' Marriage wasn't just a question of *lef*. He had had more than enough time. What did he intend to do about it?

She was alluding to the *xala*. El Hadji did not reply. He was remembering the *seet-katt*'s words: 'It is someone close to you.'

That same day, after leaving El Hadji, Yay Bineta moved out with the third wife. The women hired a taxi, filled it with furniture and crockery and drove off, leaving the doors of the villa wide open. In accordance with the saying the wife was not leaving empty-handed, for want of sexual satisfaction.

Without warning her husband Oumi N'Doye, the second wife, took her children and went to live with her parents in a poor district of the town. The bailiffs had come one morning and casually informed her that they would be back the next morning to take possession. Being a prudent woman, under cover of darkness and with the help of brothers, sisters, and cousins, she too had emptied her villa, going so far as to remove even the curtains, the fridge, and the carpets. Her father's house was too small to contain all her furniture and other household goods. For the children, used to comfort, the grand-

102

parents' slum house, the smallness of the rooms, the sandy yard, the meals taken sitting on a mat – meals which consisted every day, morning and evening, of rice eaten together from a single dish – were constant sources of friction between themselves and their cousins. Mariem openly quarrelled with her mother about the need to use public transport, the food, the lack of quiet to do her work, the fleas and the bugs. Slowly the family cohesion they had known when they lived in the 'Villa Oumi N'Doye' disintegrated. The eldest boy talked of giving up his studies at the secondary school to join the police or the army.

Oumi N'Doye badgered her husband to face up to his children's future. But El Hadji was without work and did not know what to do.

'Take them to live with you at Adja Awa Astou's,' suggested Oumi N'Doye.

When on his return to Adja Awa Astou's El Hadji raised the subject with his first wife in front of his daughter, Rama fiercely opposed the idea arguing:

'We can't afford it. This house belongs to our mother. It is out of the question to have our half-brothers and sisters here.'

Adja Awa Astou was hurt by her daughter's hard words but deep down she realized she was right. Their present situation did not augur well for the days to come.

Reduced to a cypher, El Hadji no longer visited his second wife.

Now that she had fallen from her former position of economic superiority, Oumi N'Doye tried to show she was a modern woman by going from office to office, firm to firm, in search of work. Through her change of fortune, too, she came to meet men who liked the easy life, men who could provide pleasure while they had money. So Oumi N'Doye often went out in the evening.

The sun and the moon played chase, weaving life. One day El Hadji Abdou Kader Beye was summoned to a meeting at the home of his third wife's parents. N'Gone wanted to 'take back her freedom', in the words of the consecrated formula. Modu accompanied his former employer, as a friend. They drove to old Babacar's home in Rama's Fiat.

In the all-purpose living-room were gathered three notables, members of the parish, the girl's mother and Yay Bineta. The men were those who had attended the marriage ceremony in the mosque.

In a corner of the room near the window stood the tailor's dummy, still wearing the wedding dress.

'El Hadji, you must realize, or at least you must have guessed the reason for this meeting. N'Gone wants to take back her freedom,' began the sacristan.

'We are not going to waste time on that aspect of the affair,' said Yay Bineta, the Badyen, interrupting him. She spoke in a sarcastic voice that sounded like a trumpet, her eyes gleaming with determination. 'We married our daughter, an innocent young girl, to El Hadji Abdou Kader Beye. And for four months El Hadji has been unable to prove himself a man. Since his wedding day he has avoided us. He has hidden from us day and night. Then he left us without water and electricity. But it's not this that we hold against him. We are so ashamed of the way this marriage has turned out that no one in this family dares go out during the day. So now we ask him for our freedom.'

Modu looked the Badyen up and down critically, suppressing the words of contempt that rose to his lips. The woman reminded him of an aunt, nicknamed 'The Termite' because she eroded people from the inside, only leaving the shell. In an attempt to act as a moderating influence, he said.

'Yay Bineta, you solve nothing talking like that. Yalla likes the truth only. El Hadji has not repudiated N'Gone. That is the truth! If since his marriage with your daughter El Hadji. . .'

'Say straight out that El Hadji is not a man,' said Yay Bineta interrupting him.

'That could happen to any man. Unfortunately it happened that El Hadji caught this *xala* from your daughter.'

'Do you say we are responsible?'

'Don't you accuse us,' yelled the mother, shaking her fist in Modu's face. 'If you are not men. . . In fact, were you ever men? You don't keep a girl as if she were a gold coin. Even with a gold coin you do business.'

Modu did not reply. He was seething with anger. He kept himself under control. Born as he was where the spoken word is a red-hot iron, he said right out in Wolof:

'You seem determined to take back your freedom whatever the cost. When you left you took everything with you.'

'Ah! Ah! I was expecting that. However long it stays in the river the tree-trunk will never turn into a crocodile. What did we take? The car? You hadn't paid for it. Go and see "Automobile Credit" about that. The clothes? There they are.'

The Badyen pointed to the tailor's dummy.

'Bineta, you are exceeding the bounds of politeness,' said the sacristan firmly, interrupting her. 'I will speak to El Hadji. El Hadji Abdou Kader Beye, your wife N'Gone asks you to give her her freedom. There is no need for me to explain the reason for this request.'

El Hadji drew back. He stared at his fingers.

There was a long silence.

'El Hadji, we are listening to you,' said another notable finally. He wore a fez with a red pompom. He continued: 'According to Koranic marriage law, this woman has every right to demand this separation. No one can force her to remain your wife, especially as you are unable to make her your wife.'

'For our part,' replied Modu, speaking for El Hadji, 'we do not dispute her right nor the principle. May I point out to you, however, that in our presence and in this very house the verdict has already been given: divorce.'

'What do you want? To be reimbursed?'

'Yay Bineta, you don't have the means to reimburse us. When did you see the termite offer hospitality to the tortoise?'

'You are only a servant, Modu. Your place is not here among us.'

Modu looked with compassion at El Hadji.

These quarrels had no meaning for El Hadji. At least, he did not see their relevance. He looked on without taking anything in. The tailor's dummy wearing the wedding dress and crown meant nothing to him now. Nothing at all. He could barely remember the choosing of the material, his conversations with N'Gone, what he had felt for her. It seemed to him he no longer had any feelings at all. He wanted to speak, to say something, but his words could not find their way past his throat.

'El Hadji, tell us what you intend doing? Divorce or not?' the sacristan asked him.

El Hadji looked round slowly at each of them in turn. They waited.

All at once El Hadji rose to his feet. Modu followed him outside.

They had got into the Fiat when Yay Bineta, the Badyen, came out and somehow managed to thrust the tailor's dummy onto El Hadji's lap.

'Take what you have left,' she said.

The two men said nothing.

Towards them came N'Gone, holding hands with a young man in a tight-fitting shirt, his trousers moulding his thighs. They went into the house.

The car drove off, taking the tailor's dummy with it.

They went to the shop. The shop was under seal: closed because of bankruptcy. On the corner the beggar was chanting as usual. Modu drew up alongside him. The chauffeur explained to El Hadji that the beggar could cure his *xala*. They discussed it. Modu got out of the car and went and knelt in front of the beggar. After a while Modu returned to the car and they drove off.

In a sharp, rising voice the beggar intoned his chant.

*   *   *

Two days later.

The garbage-collection lorry was doing its morning round, stopping in front of each villa. Two policemen were strolling down the street. In his makeshift shop the grocer was selling a loaf of bread to a customer. Behind the brightly coloured bougainvillæa hedges, the garden sprinklers were at work here and there wetting the pavement as well. The servants were collecting the empty dustbins.

At this early morning hour the suburb breathed with the well-being of its peaceful existence.

A maid with a little girl trotting by her side reached the fork in the road. Immediately the child let out a scream of fear and clung to the maid. Then they both screamed. Their sharp cries alerted the neighbourhood. Doors and windows opened and were immediately shut again. The woman and the child overcame their terror and took to their heels, calling for help. Dogs barked and ran away.

The two policemen hurried to the crossing. They stopped short, then reached instinctively for their revolvers and backed slowly away.

'Inform the station right away. Go on! It's a riot,' ordered the one who seemed to be in charge.

The second policeman obeyed.

The grocer hastily pushed his customer out of the door and shut his shop. The customer replaced his wallet in his pocket and hurried off.

Walking abreast across the entire width of the road came a procession of lame and blind people, lepers, legless cripples, one-legged cripples, men, women, and children, led by the beggar. There was something repulsive about the procession, which gave off a fetid smell of ragged clothes.

The policeman, his hand on his revolver, was pushed up against a hedge. As they filed past him, he shivered with repugnance and disgust.

Outside the 'Villa Adja Awa Astou' the beggar rang the bell. Then rang again. A pause. The maid opened the door. She drew back startled, nearly falling over onto the steps. Leading the way, the beggar pushed open the door, followed by his retinue. Some struggled crawling on to the verandah. They went into the sitting-room and settled themselves down as if it belonged to them. A legless cripple, his palms and knees covered with black soil from the garden, printed a black trail on the floor like a giant snail. With his strong arms he hoisted himself up into a red velvet armchair, where he sat with a foolish, triumphant grin that revealed his broken teeth and his pendulous lower lip. Another with a maggoty face and a hole where his nose had been, his deformed, scarred body visible through his rags, grabbed a white shirt and putting it on admired himself in a mirror, roaring with laughter at the reflection of his own antics. A woman with twins, emboldened by the others, tore open a cushion on the settee and wrapped one of her babies in the material. On the other cushion she rested a foot with a cloven heel and stunted toes. A hunchback walked warily round the tailor's dummy. He undressed it, placing the crown on his flat, rachitic's head. Very taken with the effect, he cried out joyfully:

'Look at me!'

A cripple with a degenerate's head and runny eyes stuffed the crockery into a sling bag. Opposite him a one-armed man was using his remaining limb to heap in front of him all the shiny objects he could find.

Entering the sitting-room, Adja Awa Astou and El Hadji Abdou Kader Beye were made speechless by the strange scene.

108

'It is me, with my friends,' said the beggar, introducing himself to El Hadji.

The sight of all these bodies kept them rooted to the spot. Adja Awa Astou was like a statue fixed to the ground, incapable of uttering a word. A legless man ran a hand over her calves. The horror sent a shiver of disgust up to the roots of her hair. Nausea spread through her whole body. A woman with a limp suddenly snatched off her headscarf and put it on her own head, provoking general hilarity. In a reflex of self-defence, Adja Awa Astou moved forward, but El Hadji held her back. Struck dumb by such audacity, he himself just looked on without reacting. He stared at the beggar in paralysed astonishment.

'Say nothing! Nothing at all, if you want to be cured,' admonished the beggar, talking as if he was in the habit of organizing such operations.

A one-legged man chanced upon the food. He hopped victoriously to a chair. He had barely sat down when two other hands eaten up with leprosy were plunged into the plate. The twins' mother begged:

'Give some to the children.'

They passed her handfuls of food, which she shared out to her children. A legless man sucked a tin of condensed milk, his eyes closed. Next to him a little boy was tying saucepans together. A leper, after suspiciously examining the bottles of mineral water, emptied them of their contents and placed them in a basket.

'I know a shop where they buy these bottles,' he told his neighbour in a nasal voice.

'What's in the bottles?' asked the neighbour.

'Do you know?'

'I'm a Muslim. I don't drink.'

'These people are criminals! Alcoholics!' declared the leper with great seriousness.

Near the large, opened fridge, an adolescent who moved along sideways like a pyramid crab grabbed a pot of yoghourt and pulled off the top. First he tasted it with his index finger. Convinced that it was edible, he lay on his back, his right hip sticking out, opened his mouth and poured the yoghourt greedily into it. Then he gestured to another lad to do likewise. The new arrival pulled his leg along as he walked. An infected sore on his shin, covered with a zinc plate held in

109

place by a piece of string, gave off a smell of rotting flesh. He seized a packet of butter and hurried away from the fridge.

'Help me! Help me!'

It was the moving 'trunk', who was determined to get onto the bed. They helped him by throwing him onto it. He disappeared among the bedclothes like a drowning man in the sea. He stuck out his head and decided to try a few somersaults. He bounced up and down, emitting incoherent shouts of joy each time he fell back.

Rama came out of her room in her nightdress. She was accosted by two hideous fellows who eyed her figure with desire and refused to leave her alone. She went to her mother. They looked at one another in puzzlement.

El Hadji Abdou Kader Beye protested.

'They're a lot of brigands.'

'No, I am taking my payment,' said the leader, who had not moved from his place.

'What for?'

'What for? Precisely! Why that *xala*? I want my payment in advance.'

'You are a lot of thieves! I am going to call the police,' said El Hadji.

His face was a mask of fear. That man reminded him of something but he could not remember what.

At the word 'police' there was a general scramble. A wind of fear passed over the faces. A fellow with a large albugo spot on his eye stopped stirring his plate in a gesture of fright. He squinted in all directions like a kid goat, looking for a way out.

'If you want to be normal again, you will obey me. You have nothing left. Nothing at all, except for your *xala*. Do you recognize me? Of course you don't.'

He went and stood in the middle of the room. His words dropping into the silence, he spoke again:

'Our story goes back a long way. It was shortly before your marriage to that woman there. Don't you remember? I was sure you would not. What I am now is your fault. Do you remember selling a large piece of land at Jeko belonging to our clan? After falsifying the clan names with the complicity of people in high places, you took our land from us. In spite of our protests, our proof of ownership, we lost

110

our case in the courts. Not satisfied with taking our land you had me thrown into prison. Why?'

The question was left unanswered. Before continuing the beggar backed up to the table. Big drops of sweat formed on his forehead and ran down his neck, following the folds of his skin. He coughed. A loose cough accompanied by a whistling noise. He was about to spit, looked around intently, and swallowed instead. He said nothing for a while, keeping his head lowered, then he looked up.

'Why? Simply because you had robbed us. Robbed us with all the appearance of legality. Because your father was the chief of the clan and the title deed for the land was in his name. But you, you knew that land did not belong only to your father and your family. When I left prison I went to see you. There was another battle and once again I was well and truly beaten by your powerful friends. People like you live on theft.'

'And exploit the poor,' thundered another voice.

'All your past wealth – for you have nothing left – was acquired by cheating. You and your colleagues build on the misfortunes of honest, ordinary people. To give yourselves clean consciences, you found charities, or you give alms at street corners to people reduced to poverty. And when we get too numerous, you call the police. . .'

'To get rid of us, as your clear your bowels,' said the fellow with the albugo in his eye, speaking fast, his arm stretched out menacingly.

'Look! Look! What am I?' asked the mother of the twins, placing herself in front of Adja Awa Astou. Replying to her own question: 'A woman, you say? No, a reproduction machine. And these babies, what will their days bring them? Look at them!'

With her right hand, she held Adja Awa Astou by the chin.

'And me? I'll never be a man. Someone like yourself knocked me down with his car. He drove off, leaving me lying there.'

An outburst of blood-curdling laughter broke the moment of calm. The leper stood on the settee and proclaimed in his nasal voice:

'I am a leper! I am a leper to myself alone. To no one else. But you, you are a disease that is infectious to everyone. The virus of a collective leprosy!'

In despair, Adja Awa Astou unrolled her beads and began praying, supported by Rama. Rama herself was bursting with anger. Against whom? Against her father? Against these wretched people? She who was always ready with the words 'revolution' and 'new social order' felt deep within her breast something like a stone falling heavily into her heart, crushing her. She could not take her eyes off her father.

'If you want to be cured, you are going to strip yourself naked, completely naked, El Hadji. Naked before us all. And each of us will spit three times on you. You have the key to your cure. Make up your mind. I can tell you now, it was I who caused your *xala*.'

Nearly two minutes went by in complete silence. El Hadji had listened carefully. He thought of the *seet-katt* who had told him: 'It is someone close to you.'

The police siren could be heard approaching. A screech of brakes followed by the clatter of feet and strident blows of a whistle broke the silence.

The muffled oriental door-bell rang.

The human wrecks clustered together, their faces stricken with fear. The mother of the twins, in a single gesture, almost a reflex action, flung one child skilfully on her back and took the other in her arms. The leper took a few paces towards the window and put his hand on the handle. The human trunk on his roller focused on a way out through a forest of twisted legs.

'What shall we do?' asked one of them, pulling off the clothes he had stolen.

They all asked the same question.

'We will all be taken to prison.'

'Don't move,' ordered the beggar. 'We are El Hadji's guests. He wants to be cured.'

A police officer pushed open the door. Behind him in the doorway could be seen other men in peaked hats. They were holding their noses.

'Good day, El Hadji,' said the senior officer in French. 'What is going on here?'

None of the faces told him anything.

'Nothing, officer,' replied Rama.

'What do you mean, nothing?'

Rama went up to the policeman.

'They are father's guests. Once a month father gives alms to the poor.'

112

The officer was not convinced.

'We have had phone calls from your neighbours complaining about a riot.'

'It is not so. See for yourself. It is I who am entertaining them,' said El Hadji.

'All right then. We respect private property. We will stay outside,' said the officer, withdrawing with his acolytes.

Outside they surrounded the villa.

'I want to leave,' announced the small man with the running sore.

'You saw for yourselves that we said nothing to the police. You are going to leave! You will spit on no one. If you refuse I will call the police back,' said Rama to the beggar.

'Daughter, don't you know that in this country the man who is in gaol is better off than the worker or the peasant? No taxes to pay and in addition you are fed, lodged, and cared for. El Hadji, we are waiting for you to decide.'

There was a pause. El Hadji glanced at his wife and daughter.

They waited.

Someone pushed a chair towards El Hadji.

'Get up!' he ordered.

All eyes were turned towards him. Everyone seemed to be holding their breath. Slowly, first one foot and then the other, El Hadji climbed onto the chair. From his greater height, he looked round at them.

'If you want to be a man again you must do what I tell you.'

'And if it is not true?' Rama asked him.

'I have not asked for any money. You can take it or leave it. El Hadji, you must choose.'

Methodically El Hadji unbuttoned his pyjama jacket. The first spittle struck him in the face.

'You must not wipe it off.'

Adja Awa Astou lowered her eyes. She was crying. A female cripple pushed her and said coarsely:

'Spit if you want him to stuff you again.'

Rama struck the woman so that she fell next to the human trunk. Two stumps with stubs of fingers formed a barrier between mother and daughter. The leper filled his mouth with saliva and shot it adroitly at El Hadji. The female cripple who had been knocked down

113

got up and gave Rama a resounding slap. Then she took her time before discharging the contents of her mouth at El Hadji.

'Your turn now, to please your mother.'

Both Adja Awa Astou and Rama were weeping.

El Hadji's face was running with spittle.

He had taken off his pyjama trousers. They were passed around from hand to hand like a trophy.

The man who had taken the wedding crown placed it on El Hadji's head.

The tumult grew louder.

Outside the forces of order raised their weapons into the firing position.

114